Hendrik Willem Van Loon

Ancient Man - The Beginning of Civilizations

I0661442

Outlook

Hendrik Willem Van Loon

Ancient Man - The Beginning of Civilizations

1. Auflage | ISBN: 978-3-73262-319-8

Erscheinungsort: Frankfurt am Main, Deutschland

Erscheinungsjahr: 2018

Outlook Verlag GmbH, Frankfurt.

Reproduction of the original.

Hendrik Willem Van Loon

Ancient Man - The Beginning of Civilizations

Outlook

ANCIENT MAN
THE BEGINNING
OF CIVILIZATIONS 1922.

BY HENDRIK WILLEM VAN LOON

DEDICATION To HANSJE AND WILLEM.

My darling boys,

You are twelve and eight years old. Soon you will be grown up. You will leave home and begin your own lives. I have been thinking about that day, wondering what I could do to help you. At last, I have had an idea. The best compass is a thorough understanding of the growth and the experience of the human race. Why should I not write a special history for you?

So I took my faithful Corona and five bottles of ink and a box of matches and a bale of paper and began to work upon the first volume. If all goes well there will be eight more and they will tell you what you ought to know of the last six thousand years.

But before you start to read let me explain what I intend to do.

I am not going to present you with a textbook. Neither will it be a volume of pictures. It will not even be a regular history in the accepted sense of the word.

I shall just take both of you by the hand and together we shall wander forth to explore the intricate wilderness of the bygone ages.

I shall show you mysterious rivers which seem to come from nowhere and which are doomed to reach no ultimate destination.

I shall bring you close to dangerous abysses, hidden carefully beneath a thick overgrowth of pleasant but deceiving romance.

Here and there we shall leave the beaten track to scale a solitary and lonely peak, towering high above the surrounding country.

Unless we are very lucky we shall

2

sometimes lose ourselves in a sudden and dense fog of ignorance.

Wherever we go we must carry our warm cloak of human sympathy and understanding for vast tracts of land will prove to be a sterile desert—swept by icy storms of popular prejudice and personal greed and unless we come well prepared we shall forsake our faith in humanity and that, dear boys, would be the worst thing that could happen to any of us.

I shall not pretend to be an infallible guide. Whenever you have a chance, take counsel with other travelers who have passed along the same route before. Compare their observations with mine and if this leads you to different conclusions, I shall certainly not be angry with you.

I have never preached to you in times gone by.

I am not going to preach to you today.

You know what the world expects of you—that you shall do your share of the common task and shall do it bravely and cheerfully.

If these books can help you, so much the better.

And with all my love I dedicate these histories to you and to the boys and girls who shall keep you company on the voyage through life.

3

HENDRIK WILLEM VAN LOON.

PREHISTORIC MAN

It took Columbus more than four weeks to sail from Spain to the West Indian Islands. We on the other hand cross the ocean in sixteen hours in a flying machine.

Five hundred years ago, three or four years were necessary to copy a book by hand. We possess linotype machines and rotary presses and we can print a new book in a couple of days.

We understand a great deal about anatomy and chemistry and mineralogy and we are familiar with a thousand different branches of science of which the very name was unknown to the people of the past.

In one respect, however, we are quite as ignorant as the most primitive of men—we do not know where we came from. We do not know how or why or when the human race began its career upon this Earth. With a million facts at our disposal we are still obliged to follow the example of the fairy-stories and begin in the old way:

"Once upon a time there was a man."

This man lived hundreds of thousands of years ago.

What did he look like?

We do not know. We never saw his picture. Deep in the clay of an ancient soil we have sometimes found a few pieces of his skeleton. They were hidden amidst masses of bones of animals that have long since disappeared from the face of the earth. We have taken these bones and they allow us to reconstruct the strange creature who happens to be our ancestor.

The great-great-grandfather of the human race was a very ugly and unattractive mammal. He was quite small. The heat of the sun and the biting wind of the cold winter had colored his skin a dark brown. His head and most of his body were covered with long hair. He had very thin but strong fingers which made his hands look like those of a monkey. His forehead was low and his jaw was like the jaw of a wild animal which uses its teeth both as fork and knife.

PREHISTORIC MAN.

He wore no clothes. He had seen no fire except the flames of the rumbling volcanoes which filled the earth with their smoke and their lava.

He lived in the damp blackness of vast forests.

When he felt the pangs of hunger he ate raw

leaves and the roots of plants or he stole the eggs from the nest of an angry bird.

Once in a while, after a long and patient chase, he managed to catch a sparrow or a small wild dog or perhaps a rabbit These he would eat raw, for prehistoric man did not know that food could be cooked.

His teeth were large and looked like the teeth of many of our own animals.

During the hours of day this primitive human being went about in search of food for himself and his wife and his young.

At night, frightened by the noise of the beasts, who were in search of prey, he would creep into a hollow tree or he would hide himself behind a few big boulders, covered with moss and great, big spiders.

In summer he was exposed to the scorching rays of the sun.

During the winter he froze with cold.

When he hurt himself (and hunting animals are for ever breaking their bones or spraining their ankles) he had no one to take care of him.

He had learned how to make certain sounds to warn his fellow-beings whenever danger threatened. In this he resembled a dog who barks when a stranger approaches. In many other respects he was far less attractive than a well-bred house pet.

Altogether, early man was a miserable creature who lived in a world of fright and hunger, who was surrounded by a thousand enemies and who was for ever haunted by the vision of friends and relatives who had been eaten up by wolves and bears and the terrible sabre-toothed tiger.

Of the earliest history of this man we know

nothing. He had no tools and he built no homes. He lived and died and left no traces of his existence. We keep track of him through his bones and they tell us that he lived more than two thousand centuries ago.

The rest is darkness.

Until we reach the time of the famous Stone Age, when man learned the first rudimentary principles of what we call civilization.

Of this Stone Age I must tell you in some detail.

THE WORLD GROWS COLD

Something was the matter with the weather.

Early man did not know what "time" meant.

He kept no records of birthdays and wedding-anniversaries or the hour of death.

He had no idea of days or weeks or years.

When the sun arose in the morning he did not say "Behold another day." He said "It is Light" and he used the rays of the early sun to gather food for his family.

When it grew dark, he returned to his wife and children, gave them part of the day's catch (some berries and a few birds), stuffed himself full with raw meat and went to sleep.

In a very general way he kept track of the seasons. Long experience had taught him that the cold Winter was invariably followed by the mild Spring—that Spring grew into the hot Summer when fruits ripened and the wild ears of corn were ready to be plucked and eaten. The Summer ended when gusts of wind swept the leaves from the trees and when a number of animals crept into their holes to make ready for the long hibernal sleep.

THE GLACIAL PERIOD.

It had always been that way. Early man accepted these useful changes of cold and warm but asked no questions. He lived and that was enough to satisfy him.

Suddenly, however, something happened that worried him greatly.

The warm days of Summer had come very late. The fruits had not ripened at all. The tops ofthe mountains which used to be covered with grass lay deeply hidden under a heavy burden of snow.

Then one morning quite a number of wild people, different from the other inhabitants of his valley had approached from the region of the

10

high peaks.

They muttered sounds which no one could understand. They looked lean and appeared to be starving. Hunger and cold seemed to have driven them from their former homes.

There was not enough food in the valley for both the old inhabitants and the newcomers. When they tried to stay more than a few days there was a terrible fight and whole families were killed. The others fled into the woods and were not seen again.

For a long time nothing occurred of any importance.

But all the while, the days grew shorter and the nights were colder than they ought to have been.

Finally, in a gap between the two high hills, there appeared a tiny speck of greenish ice. It increased in size as the years went by. Very slowly a gigantic glacier was sliding down the slopes of the mountain ridge. Huge stones were being pushed into the valley. With the noise of a dozen thunderstorms they suddenly tumbled among the frightened people and killed them while they slept. Century-old trees were crushed into kindling wood by the high walls of ice that knew of no mercy to either man or beast.

At last, it began to snow.

It snowed for months and months and months.

THE CAVE-MAN.

All the plants died. The animals fled in search of the southern sun. The valley became uninhabitable. Man hoisted his children upon his back, took the few pieces of stone which he had used as a weapon and went forth to find a new home.

Why the world should have grown cold at that particular moment, we do not know. We can not even guess at the cause.

The gradual lowering of the temperature, however, made a great difference to the human race.

For a time it looked as if every one would die. But in the end this period of suffering proved a real blessing. It killed all the weaker people and forced the survivors to sharpen their wits lest they perish, too.

Placed before the choice of hard thinking or quick dying the same brain that had first turned a stone into a hatchet now solved difficulties which had never faced the older generations.

In the first place, there was the question of clothing. It had grown much too cold to do without some sort of artificial covering. Bears and bisons and other animals who live in northern regions are protected against snow and ice by a heavy coat of fur. Man possessed no such coat. His skin was very delicate and he suffered greatly.

He solved his problem in a very simple fashion. He dug a hole and he covered it with branches and leaves and a little grass. A bear came by and fell into this artificial cave. Man waited until the creature was weak from lack of food and then killed him with many blows of a big stone. With a sharp piece of flint he cut the fur of the animal's back. Then he dried it in the sparse rays of the sun, put it around his own shoulders and enjoyed the same warmth that had formerly kept the bear happy and comfortable.

Then there was the housing problem. Many animals were in the habit of sleeping in a dark cave. Man followed their example and searched until he found an empty grotto. He shared it with bats and all sorts of creeping insects but this he did not mind. His new home kept him warm and that was enough.

Often, during a thunderstorm a tree had been hit by lightning. Sometimes the entire forest had been set on fire. Man had seen these forest-fires. When he had come too near he had been driven away by the heat. He now remembered that fire gave warmth.

Thus far, fire had been an enemy.

Now it became a friend.

A dead tree, dragged into a cave and lighted by means of smouldering branches from a burning forest filled the room with unusual but very pleasant heat.

Perhaps you will laugh. All these things seem so very simple. They are very simple to us because some one, ages and ages ago, was clever enough to think of them. But the first cave that was made comfortable by the fire of an old log attracted more attention than the first house that ever was lighted by electricity.

When at last, a specially brilliant fellow hit upon the idea of throwing raw meat into the hot ashes before eating it, he added something to the sum total of human knowledge which made the cave-man feel that the height of civilization had been reached.

Nowadays, when we hear of another marvelous invention we are very proud.

"What more," we ask, "can the human brain accomplish?"

And we smile contentedly for we live in the most remarkable of all ages and no one has ever performed such miracles as our engineers and our chemists.

Forty thousand years ago when the world was on the point of freezing to death, an unkempt and unwashed cave-man, pulling the feathers out of a half-dead chicken with the help of his brown fingers and his big white teeth—throwing the feathers and the bones upon the same floor that served him and his family as a bed, felt just as happy and just as proud when he was taught how the hot cinders of a fire would change raw meat into a delicious meal.

"What a wonderful age," he would exclaim and he would lie down amidst the decaying skeletons of the animals which had served him as his dinner and he would dream of his own perfection while bats, as large as small dogs, flew restlessly through the cave and while rats, as big as small cats, rummaged among the left overs.

Quite often the cave gave way to the pressure of the surrounding rock. Then man was hurled amidst the bones of his own victims.

Thousands of years later the anthropologist (ask your father what that means) comes along with his little spade and his wheelbarrow.

He digs and he digs and at last he uncovers this age-old tragedy and makes it possible for me to tell you all about it.

THE END OF THE STONE AGE

The struggle to keep alive during the cold period was terrible. Many races of men and animals, whose bones we have found, disappeared from the face of the earth.

Whole tribes and clans were wiped out by hunger and cold and want. First the children would die and then the parents. The old people were left to the mercy of the wild animals who hastened to occupy the undefended cave. Until another change in the climate or the slowly decreasing moisture of the air made life impossible for these wild invaders and forced them to find a retreat in the heart of theAfrican jungle where they have lived ever since.

This part of my history is very difficult because the changes which I must describe were so very slow and so very gradual.

Nature is never in a hurry. She has all eternity in which to accomplish her task and she can afford to bring about the necessary changes with deliberate care.

Prehistoric man lived through at least four definite eras when the ice descended far down into the valleys and covered the greater part of the European continent.

The last one of these periods came to an end almost thirty thousand years ago.

From that moment on man left behind him concrete evidence of his existence in the form of tools and arms and pictures and in a general way we can say that history begins when the last cold period had become a thing of the past.

The endless struggle for life had taught the survivors many things.

Stone and wooden implements had become as common as steel tools are in our own days.

Gradually the rudely chipped flint axe had been replaced by one of polished flint which was infinitely more practical. It allowed man to attack many animals at whose mercy he had been since the beginning of time.

The mammoth was no longer seen.

The musk-ox had retreated to the polar circle.

The tiger had left Europe for good.

The cave-bear no longer ate little children.

The powerful brain of the weakest and most helpless of all living creatures—Man—had devised such terrible instruments of destruction that he was now the master of all the other animals.

The first great victory over Nature had been gained but many others were to follow.

Equipped with a full set of tools both for hunting and fishing, the cave-dweller looked for new living quarters.

The shores of rivers and lakes offered the best opportunity for a regular livelihood.

The old caves were deserted and the human race moved toward the water.

Now that man could handle heavy axes, the felling of trees no longer offered any great difficulties.

For countless ages birds had been constructing comfortable houses out of chips of wood and grass amidst the branches of trees.

Man followed their example.

He, too, built himself a nest and called it this "home."

He did not, except in a few parts of Asia, take to the trees which were a bit too small and unsteady for his purpose.

He cut down a number of logs. These he drove firmly into the soft bottom of a shallow lake. On top of them he constructed a wooden platform and upon this platform he erected his first wooden house.

It offered many advantages over the old cave.

No wild animals could break into it and robbers could not enter it. The lake itself was an inexhaustible store-room containing an endless supply of fresh fish.

These houses built on piles were much healthier than the old caves and they gave the children a chance to grow up into strong men. The population increased steadily and man began to occupy vast tracts of wilderness which had been unoccupied since the beginning of time.

And all the time new inventions were made which made life more comfortable and less dangerous.

Often enough these innovations were not due to the cleverness of man's brain.

He simply copied the animals.

You know of course that there are a large number of beasties who prepare for the long winter by burying nuts and acorns and other food which is abundant during the summer. Just think of the squirrels who are for ever filling their larder in gardens and parks with supplies for the winter and the early spring.

Early man, less intelligent in many respects than the squirrels, had not known how to preserve anything for the future.

He ate until his hunger was stilled, but what he

did not need right away he allowed to rot. As a result he often went without his meals during the cold period and many of his children died from hunger and want.

Until he followed the example of the animals and prepared for the future by laying in sufficient stores when the harvest had been good and there was an abundance of wheat and grain.

We do not know which genius first discovered the use of pottery but he deserves a statue.

Very likely it was a woman who had got tired of the eternal chores of the kitchen and wanted to make her household duties a little less exacting. She noticed that chunks of clay, when exposed to the rays of the sun, got baked into a hard substance.

If a flat piece of clay could be transformed into a brick, a slightly curved piece of the same material must produce a similar result.

And behold, the brick grew into a piece of pottery and the human race was able to save for the day of tomorrow.

If you think that my praises of this invention are exaggerated, look at the breakfast table and see what pottery, in one form and the other, means in your own life.

Your oatmeal is served in a dish.

The cream is served from a pitcher.

Your eggs are carried from the kitchen to the dining-room table on a plate.

Your milk is brought to you in a china mug. Then go to the store-room (if there is no store-room in your house go to the nearest Delicatessen store). You will see how all the things which we are supposed to eat tomorrow and next week and next year have been put away in jars and cans and other artificial containers which Nature did not provide for us but which man was forced to invent and perfect before he could be assured of his regular meals all the year around.

Even a gas-tank is nothing but a large pitcher, made of iron because iron does not break as easily as china and is less porous than clay. So are barrels and bottles and pots and pans. They all serve the same purpose—of providing us in the future with those things of which we happen to have an abundance at the present moment.

And because he could preserve eatable things for the day of need, man began to raise vegetables and grain and saved the surplus for future consumption.

This explains why, during the late Stone Age, we find the first wheat-fields and the first gardens, grouped around the settlements of the early pile-dwellers.

It also tells us why man gave up his habit of wandering and settled down in one fixed spot where he raised his children until the day of his death when he was decently buried among his own people.

PREHISTORIC MAN IS DISCOVERED.

It is safe to say that these earliest ancestors of ours would have given up the ways of savages of their own accord if they had been left to their fate.

But suddenly there was an end to their isolation.

Prehistoric man was discovered.

A traveler from the unknown south-land who had dared to cross the turbulent sea and the forbidding mountain passes had found his way to the wild people of Central Europe.

On his back he carried a pack.

When he had spread his wares before the gaping curiosity of the bewildered natives, their eyes beheld wonders of which their minds had never dared to dream.

They saw bronze hammers and axes and tools made of iron and helmets made of copper and beautiful ornaments consisting of a strangely colored substance which the foreign visitor called "glass."

And overnight the Age of Stone came to an end.

It was replaced by a new civilization which had discarded wooden and stone implements centuries before and had laid the foundations for that "Age of Metal" which has endured until our own day.

It is of this new civilization that I shall tell you in the rest of my book and if you do not mind, we shall leave the northern continent for a couple of thousand years and pay a visit to Egypt and to western Asia.

"But," you will say, "this is not fair. You promise to tell us about prehistoric man and then, just when the story is going to be interesting, you close the chapter and you jump to another part of the world and we must jump with you whether we like it or not."

I know. It does not seem the right thing to do.

Unfortunately, history is not at all like mathematics.

When you solve a sum you go from "a" to "b" and from "b" to "c" and from "c" to "d" and so on.

History on the other hand jumps from "a" to "z" and then back to "f" and next to "m" without any apparent respect for neatness and order.

There is a good reason for this.

History is not exactly a science.

It tells the story of the human race and most people, however much we may try to change their nature, refuse to behave with the regularity and the precision of the tables of multiplication.

No two men ever do precisely the same thing.

No two human brains ever reach exact y the same conclusion.

You will notice that for yourself when you grow up.

It was not different a few hundred centuries ago.

Prehistoric man, as I just told you, was on a fair way to progress.

He had managed to survive the ice and the snow and the wild animals and that in itself, was a great deal.

He had invented many useful things.

Suddenly, however, other people in a different part of the world entered the race.

They rushed forward at a terrible speed and within a very short space of time they reached a height of civilization which had never before been seen upon our planet. Then they set forth to teach what they knew to the others who had been less intelligent than themselves.

Now that I have explained this to you, does it not seem just to give the Egyptians and the people of western Asia their full share of the chapters of this book?

THE EARLIEST SCHOOL OF THE HUMAN RACE

We are the children of a practical age.

We travel from place to place in our own little locomotives which we call automobiles.

When we wish to speak to a friend whose home is a thousand miles away, we say "Hello" into a rubber tube and ask for a certain telephone number in Chicago.

At night when the room grows dark we push a button and there is light.

If we happen to be cold we push another button and the electric stove spreads its pleasant glow through our study.

On the other hand in summer when it is hot the same electric current will start a small artificial storm (an electric fan) which keeps us cool and comfortable.

We seem to be the masters of all the forces of nature and we make them work for us as if they were our very obedient slaves.

But do not forget one thing when you pride yourself upon our splendid achievements.

We have constructed the edifice of our modern civilization upon the fundament of wisdom that had been built at great pains by the people of the ancient world.

Do not be afraid of their strange names which you will meet upon every page of the coming chapters.

Babylonians and Egyptians and Chaldeans and Sumerians are all dead and gone, but they continue to influence our own lives in everything we do, in the letters we write, in the language we use, in the complicated mathematical problems which we must solve before we can build a bridge or a skyscraper.

And they deserve our grateful respect as long as our planet continues to race through the wide space of the high heavens.

These ancient people of whom I shall now tell you lived in three definite spots.

Two of these were found along the banks of vast rivers.

The third was situated on the shores of the Mediterranean.

The oldest center of civilization developed in the valley of the Nile, in a country which was called Egypt.

The second was located in the fertile plains between two big rivers of western Asia, to which the ancients gave the name of Mesopotamia.

The third one which you will find along the shore of the Mediterranean, was inhabited by the Phoenicians, the earliest of all colonizers and by the Jews who bestowed upon the rest of the world the main principles of their moral laws.

This third center of civilization is known by its ancient Babylonian name of Suri, or as we pronounce it, Syria.

The history of the people who lived in these regions covers more than five thousand years.

It is a very, very complicated story.

I can not give you many details.

I shall try and weave their adventures into a single fabric, which will look like one of those marvelous rugs of which you read in the tales which Scheherazade told to Harun the Just.

THE KEY OF STONE

Fifty years before the birth of Christ, the Romans conquered the land along the eastern shores of the Mediterranean and among this newly acquired territory was a country called Egypt.

The Romans, who are to play such a great role in our history, were a race of practical men.

They built bridges, they constructed roads, and with a small but highly trained army of soldiers and civil officers, they managed to rule the greater part of Europe, of eastern Africa and western Asia.

As for art and the sciences, these did not interest them very much. They regarded with suspicion a man who could play the lute or who could write a poem about Spring and only thought him little better than the clever fellow who could walk the tightrope or who had trained his poodle dog to stand on its hind legs. They left such things to the Greeks and to the Orientals, both of whom they despised, while they themselves spent their days and nights keeping order among the thousand and one nations of their vast empire.

When they first set foot in Egypt that country was already terribly old.

More than six thousand and five hundred years had gone by since the history of the Egyptian people had begun.

Long before any one had dreamed of building a city amidst the swamps of the river Tiber, the kings of Egypt had ruled far and wide and had made their court the center of all civilization.

While the Romans were still savages who chased

wolves and bears with clumsy stone axes, the Egyptians were writing books, performing intricate medical operations and teaching their children the tables of multiplication.

This great progress they owed chiefly to one very wonderful invention, to the art of preserving their spoken words and their ideas for the benefit of their children and grandchildren.

We call this the art of writing.

We are so familiar with writing that we can not understand how people ever managed to live without books and newspapers and magazines.

But they did and it was the main reason why they made such slow progress during the first million years of their stay upon this planet.

They were like cats and dogs who can only teach their puppies and their kittens a few simple things (barking at a stranger and climbing trees and such things) and who, because they can not write, possess no way in which they can use the experience of their countless ancestors.

This sounds almost funny, doesn't it?

And why make such a fuss about so simple a matter?

But did you ever stop to think what happens when you write a letter?

Suppose that you are taking a trip in the mountains and you have seen a deer.

You want to tell this to your father who is in the city.

What do you do?

You put a lot of dots and dashes upon a piece of paper—you add a few more dots and dashes upon an envelope and you carry your epistle to the mailbox together with a two-cent stamp.

What have you really been doing?

You have changed a number of spoken words into a number of pothooks and scrawls.

But how did you know how to make your curlycues in such a fashion that both the postman and your father could retranslate them into spoken words?

You knew, because some one had taught you how to draw the precise figures which represented the sound of your spoken words.

Just take a few letters and see the way this game is played.

We make a guttural noise and write down a "G."

We let the air pass through our closed teeth and we write down "S."

We open our mouth wide and make a noise like a steam engine and the sound is written down "H."

It took the human race hundreds of thousands of years to discover this and the credit for it goes to the Egyptians.

Of course they did not use the letters which have been used to print this book.

They had a system of their own.

It was much prettier than ours but not quite so simple.

It consisted of little figures and images of things around the house and around the farm, of knives and plows and birds and pots and pans. These little figures their scribes scratched and painted upon the wall of the temples, upon the coffins of their dead kings and upon the dried leaves of the papyrus plant which has given its name to our "paper."

But when the Romans entered this vast library they showed neither enthusiasm nor interest.

They possessed a system of writing of their own which they thought vastly superior.

THE KEY OF STONE.

They did not know that the Greeks (from whom they had learned their alphabet) had in turn obtained theirs from the Phoenicians who had again borrowed with great success from the old Egyptians. They did not know and they did not care. In their schools the Roman alphabet was taught exclusively and what was good enough for the Roman children was good enough for everybody else.

You will understand that the Egyptian language did not long survive the indifference and the opposition of the Roman governors. It was forgotten. It died just as the languages of most of our Indian tribes have become a thing of the past.

The Arabs and the Turks who succeeded the Romans as the rulers of Egypt abhorred all writing that was not connected with their holy book, the Koran.

At last in the middle of the sixteenth century a few western visitors came to Egypt and showed a mild interest in these strange pictures.

But there was no one to explain their meaning and these first Europeans were as wise as the Romans and the Turks had been before them.

Now it happened, late in the eighteenth century that a certain French general by the name of Buonaparte visited Egypt. He did not go there to study ancient history. He wanted to use the country as a starting point for a military expedition against the British colonies in India. This expedition failed completely but it helped solve the mysterious problem of the ancient Egyptian writing.

Among the soldiers of Napoleon Buonaparte there was a young officer by the name of Broussard. He was stationed at the fortress of St. Julien on the western mouth of the Nile which is called the Rosetta river.

Broussard liked to rummage among the ruins of the lower Nile and one day he found a stone which greatly puzzled him.

Like everything else in that neighborhood, it was covered with picture writing.

But this slab of black basalt was different from anything that had ever been discovered.

It carried three inscriptions and one of these (oh

joy!) was in Greek.

The Greek language was known.

As it was almost certain that the Egyptian part contained a translation of the Greek (or vice versa), the key to ancient Egyptian seemed to have been discovered.

But it took more than thirty years of very hard work before the key had been made to fit the lock.

Then the mysterious door was opened and the ancient treasure house of Egypt was forced to surrender its secrets.

The man who gave his life to the task of deciphering this language was Jean Francois Champollion—usually called Champollion Junior to distinguish him from his older brother who was also a very learned man.

Champollion Junior was a baby when the French revolution broke out and therefore he escaped serving in the armies of the General Buonaparte.

While his countrymen were marching from one glorious victory to another (and back again as such Imperial armies are apt to do) Champollion studied the language of the Copts, the native Christians of Egypt. At the age of nineteen he was appointed a professor of History at one of the smaller French universities and there he began his great work of translating the pictures of the old Egyptian language.

For this purpose he used the famous black stone of Rosetta which Broussard had discovered among the ruins near the mouth of the Nile.

The original stone was still in Egypt. Napoleon had been forced to vacate the country in a hurry and he had left this curiosity behind. When the English retook Alexandria in the year 1801 they found the stone and carried it to London, where you may see it this very day in the British Museum. The Inscriptions however had been copied and had been taken to France, where they were used by Champollion.

The Greek text was quite clear. It contained the story of Ptolemy V and his wife Cleopatra, the grandmother of that other Cleopatra about whom Shakespeare wrote. The other two inscriptions, however, refused to surrender their secrets.

One of them was in hieroglyphics, the name we give to the oldest known Egyptian writing. The word Hieroglyphic is Greek and means "sacred carving." It is a very good name for it fully describes the purpose and nature of this script. The priests who had invented this art did not want the common people to become too familiar with the deep mysteries of preserving speech. They made writing a sacred business.

They surrounded it with much mystery and decreed that the carving of hieroglyphics be regarded as a sacred art and forbade the people to practice it for such a common purpose as business or commerce.

They could enforce this rule with success so long as the country was inhabited by simple farmers who lived at home and grew everything they needed upon their own fields. But gradually Egypt became a land of traders and these traders needed a means of communication beyond the spoken word. So they boldly took the little figures of the priests and simp ified them for their own purposes. Thereafter they wrote their business letters in the new script which became known as the "popular language" and which we call by its Greek name, the "Demotic language."

The Rosetta stone carried both the sacred and the popular translations of the Greek text and upon these two Champollion centered his attack. He collected every piece of Egyptian script which he could get and together with the Rosetta stone he compared and studied them until after twenty years of patient drudgery he understood the meaning of fourteen little figures.

That means that he spent more than a whole year to decipher each single picture.

Finally he went to Egypt and in the year 1823 he printed the first scientific book upon the subject of the ancient hieroglyphics.

Nine years later he died from overwork, as a true martyr to the great task which he had set himself as a boy.

His work, however, lived after him.

Others continued his studies and today Egyptologists can read hieroglyphics as easily as we can read the printed pages of our newspapers.

Fourteen pictures in twenty years seems very slow work. But let me tell you something of Champollion's difficulties. Then you will understand, and understanding, you will admire his courage.

The old Egyptians did not use a simple sign language. They had passed beyond that stage.

Of course, you know what sign language is.

Every Indian story has a chapter about queer messages, written in the form of little pictures. Hardly a boy but at some stage or other of his life, as a buffalo hunter or an Indian fighter, has invented a sign language of his own, and all Boy Scouts are familiar with it. But Egyptian was something quite different and I must try and make this clear to you with a few pictures. Suppose that you were Champollion and that you were reading an old papyrus which told the story of a farmer who lived somewhere along the banks of the river Nile.

Suddenly you came across a picture of a man with a saw.

"Very well," you said, "that means, of course, that the farmer went out and cut a tree down." Most likely you had guessed correctly.

Next you took another page of hieroglyphics.

They told the story of a queen who had lived to be eighty-two years old. Right in the middle of the text the same picture occurred. That was very puzzling, to say the least. Queens do not go about cutting down trees. They let other people do it for them. A young queen may saw wood for the sake of exercise, but a queen of eighty-two stays at home with her cat and her spinning wheel. Yet, the picture was there. The ancient priest who drew it must have placed it there for a definite purpose.

What could he have meant?

That was the riddle which Champollion finally solved.

He discovered that the Egyptians were the first people to use what we call "phonetic writing."

Like most other words which express a scientific idea, the word "phonetic" is of Greek origin. It means the "science of the sound which is made by our speech." You have seen the Greek word "phone," which means the voice, before. It occurs in our word "telephone," the machine which carries the voice to a distant point.

Ancient Egyptian was "phonetic" and it set man free from the narrow limits of that sign language which in some primitive form had been used ever since the cave-dweller began to scratch pictures of wild animals upon the walls of his home.

Now let us return for a moment to the little fellow with his saw who suddenly appeared in the story of the old queen. Evidently he had something to do with a saw.

A "saw" is either a tool which you find in a carpenter shop or it means the past tense of the verb "to see."

This is what had happened to the word during the course of many centuries.

First of all it had meant a man with a saw.

Then it came to mean the sound which we reproduce by the three modern letters, s, a and w. In the end the original meaning of carpentering was lost entirely and the picture indicated the past tense of "to see."

A modern English sentence done into the images of ancient Egypt will show you what I mean.

The ![eye symbol] means either these two round objects in your head which allow you to see, or it means "I," the person who is talking or writing.

A ![bee symbol] is either an animal which gathers honey and pricks you in the finger when you try to catch it, or it represents to verb "to be," which is pronounced the same way and which means to "exist." Again it may be the first part of a verb like "be-come" or "be-have." In this case the bee is followed by a ![leaf symbol] which represents the sound which we find in the word "leave" or "leaf." Put your "bee" and your "leaf" together and you have the two sounds which make the verb "bee-leave" or "believe" as we write it nowadays.

The "eye" you know all about.

Finally you get a picture which looks like a giraffe. ![giraffe symbol] It is a giraffe, and it is part of the old sign language, which has been continued wherever it seemed most convenient.

Therefore you get the following sentence, "I believe I saw a giraffe."

This system, once invented, was developed during thousands of years.

37

Gradually the most important figures came to mean single letters or short sounds like "fu" or "em" or "dee" or "zee," or as we write them, f and m and d and z. And with the help of these, the Egyptians could write anything they wanted upon every conceivable subject, and could preserve the experience of one generation for the benefit of the next without the slightest difficulty.

That, in a very general way, is what Champollion taught us after the exhausting search which killed him when he was a young man.

That too, is the reason why today we know Egyptian history better than that of any other ancient country.

———————————

THE LAND OF THE LIVING AND THE LAND OF THE DEAD

The History of Man is the record of a hungry creature in search of food.

Wherever food was plentiful and easily gathered, thither man travelled to make his home.

The fame of the Nile valley must have spread at an early date. From far and wide, wild people flocked to the banks of the river. Surrounded on all sides by desert or sea, it was not easy to reach these fertile fields and only the hardiest men and women survived.

We do not know who they were. Some came from the interior of Africa and had woolly hair and thick lips.

Others, with a yellowish skin, came from the desert of Arabia and the broad rivers of western Asia.

They fought each other for the possession of this wonderful land.

They built villages which their neighbors destroyed and they rebuilt them with the bricks they had taken from other neighbors whom they in turn had vanquished.

Gradually a new race developed. They called themselves "remi," which means simply "the Men." There was a touch of pride in this name and they used it in the same sense that we refer to America as "God's own country."

Part of the year, during the annual flood of the Nile, they lived on small islands within a country which itself was cut off from the rest of the world by the sea and the desert. No wonder that these people were what we call "insular," and had the habits of villagers who rarely come in contact with their neighbors.

They liked their own ways best. They thought their own habits and customs just a trifle better than those of anybody else. In the same way, their own gods were considered more powerful than the gods of other nations. They did not exactly despise foreigners, but they felt a mild pity for them and if possible they kept them outside of the Egyptian domains, lest their own people be corrupted by "foreign notions."

They were kind-hearted and rarely did anything that was cruel. They were patient and in business dealings they were rather indifferent Life came as an easy gift and they never became stingy and mean like northern people who have to struggle for mere existence.

When the sun arose above the blood-red horizon of the distant desert, they went forth to till their fields. When the last rays of light had disappeared beyond the mountain ridges, they went to bed.

They worked hard, they plodded and they bore whatever happened with stolid unconcern and profound patience.

They believed that this life was but a short preface to a new existence which began the moment Death had entered the house. Until at last, the life of the future came to be regarded as more important than the life of the present and the people of Egypt turned their teeming land into one vast shrine for the worship of the dead.

THE LAND OF THE DEAD.

And as most of the papyrus-rolls of the ancient valley tell stories of a religious nature we know with great accuracy just what gods the Egyptians revered and how they tried to assure all possible happiness and comfort to those who had entered upon the eternal sleep. In the beginning each little village had possessed a god of its own.

Often this god was supposed to reside in a queerly shaped stone or in the branch of a particularly large tree. It was well to be good friends with him for he could do great harm and destroy the harvest and prolong the period of drought until the people and the cattle had all died of thirst. Therefore the villages made him presents—offered him things to eat or a bunch of flowers.

When the Egyptians went forth to fight their enemies the god must needs be taken along, until he became a sort of battle flag around which the people rallied in time of danger.

But when the country grew older and better roads had been built and the Egyptians had begun to travel, the old "fetishes," as such chunks of stone and wood were called, lost their importance and were thrown away or were left in a neglected corner or were used as doorsteps or chairs.

Their place was taken by new gods who were more powerful than the old ones had been and who represented those forces of nature which influenced the lives of the Egyptians of the entire valley.

First among these was the Sun which makes all things grow.

Next came the river Nile which tempered the heat of the day and brought rich deposits of clay to refresh the fields and make them fertile.

Then there was the kindly Moon which at night rowed her little boat across the arch of heaven and there was Thunder and there was Lightning and there were any number of things which could make life happy or miserable according to their pleasure and desire.

Ancient man, entirely at the mercy of these forces of nature, could not get rid of them as easily as we do when we plant lightning rods upon our houses or build reservoirs which keep us alive during the summer months when there is no rain.

On the contrary they formed an intimate part of his daily life—they accompanied him from the moment he was put into his cradle until the day that his body was prepared for eternal rest.

Neither could he imagine that such vast and powerful phenomena as a bolt of lightning or the flood of a river were mere impersonal things. Some one—somewhere—must be their master and must direct them as the engineer directs his engine or a captain steers his ship.

A God-in-Chief was therefore created, like the commanding general of an army.

A number of lower officers were placed at his disposal.

Within their own territory each one could act independently.

In grave matters, however, which affected the happiness of all the people, they must take orders from their master.

The Supreme Divine Ruler of the land of Egypt was called Osiris, and all the little Egyptian children knew the story of his wonderful life.

Once upon a time, in the valley of the Nile, there lived a king called Osiris.

He was a good man who taught his subjects how to till their fields and who gave his country just laws. But he had a bad brother whose name was Seth.

Now Seth envied Osiris because he was so virtuous and one day he invited him to dinner and afterwards he said that he would like to show him something. Curious Osiris asked what it was and Seth said that it was a funnily shaped coffin which fitted one like a suit of clothes. Osiris said that he would like to try it. So he lay down in the coffin but no sooner was he inside when bang!—Seth shut the lid. Then he called for his servants and ordered them to throw the coffin into the Nile.

Soon the news of his terrible deed spread
throughout the land. Isis, the wife of Osiris, who
had loved her husband very dearly, went at once
to the banks of the Nile, and after a short while
the waves threw the coffin upon the shore. Then
she went forth to tell her son Horus, who ruled
in another land, but no sooner had she left than
Seth, the wicked brother, broke into the palace
and cut the body of Osiris into fourteen pieces.

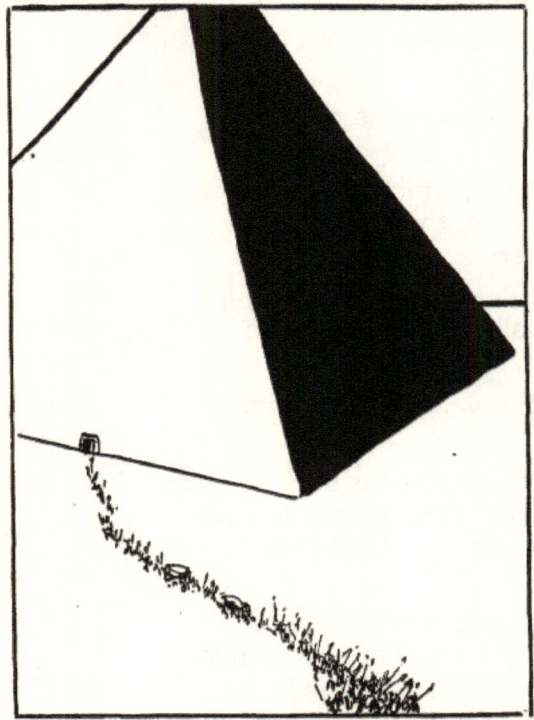

A PYRAMID.

When Isis returned, she discovered what Seth
had done. She took the fourteen pieces of the
dead body and sewed them together and then
Osiris came back to life and reigned for ever and
ever as king of the lower world to which the
souls of men must travel after they have left the

body.

As for Seth, the Evil One, he tried to escape, but Horus, the son of Osiris and Isis, who had been warned by his mother, caught him and slew him.

This story of a faithful wife and a wicked brother and a dutiful son who avenged his father and the final victory of virtue over wickedness formed the basis of the religious life of the people of Egypt.

Osiris was regarded as the god of all living things which seemingly die in the winter and yet return to renewed existence the next spring. As ruler of the Life Hereafter, he was the final judge of the acts of men, and woe unto him who had been cruel and unjust and had oppressed the weak.

As for the world of the departed souls, it was situated beyond the high mountains of the west (which was also the home of the young Nile) and when an Egyptian wanted to say that someone had died, he said that he "had gone west."

Isis shared the honors and the duties of Osiris with him. Their son Horus, who was worshipped as the god of the Sun (hence the word "horizon," the place where the sun sets) became the first of a new line of Egyptian kings and all the Pharaohs of Egypt had Horus as their middle name.

Of course, each little city and every small village continued to worship a few divinities of their own. But generally speaking, all the people recognized the sublime power of Osiris and tried to gain his favor.

HOW THE PYRAMIDS GREW.

This was no easy task, and led to many strange customs. In the first place, the Egyptians came to believe that no soul could enter into the realm of Osiris without the possession of the body which had been its place of residence in this world.

Whatever happened, the body must be preserved after death, and it must be given a permanent and suitable home. Therefore as soon as a man had died, his corpse was embalmed. This was a difficult and complicated operation which was performed by an official who was half doctor and half priest, with the help of an assistant whose duty it was to make the incision through which the chest could be filled with cedar-tree pitch and myrrh and cassia. This assistant belonged to a special class of people who were counted among the most despised of men. The Egyptians thought it a terrible thing to commit acts of violence upon a human being, whether dead or living, and only the lowest of the low could be hired to perform this unpopular task.

Afterwards the priest took the body again and for a period of ten weeks he allowed it to be soaked in a solution of natron which was brought for this purpose from the distant desert of Libya. Then the body had become a "mummy" because it was filled with "Mumiai" or pitch. It was wrapped in yards and yards of specially prepared linen and it was placed in a beautifully decorated wooden coffin, ready to be removed to its final home in the western desert.

The grave itself was a little stone room in the sand of the desert or a cave in a hill-side.

After the coffin had been placed in the center the little room was well supplied with cooking utensils and weapons and statues (of clay or wood) representing bakers and butchers who were expected to wait upon their dead master in case he needed anything. Flutes and fiddles were added to give the occupant of the grave a chance to while away the long hours which he must spend in this "house of eternity."

Then the roof was covered with sand and the dead Egyptian was left to the peaceful rest of eternal sleep.

But the desert is full of wild creatures, hyenas and wolves, and they dug their way through the wooden roof and the sand and ate up the mummy.

This was a terrible thing, for then the soul was

doomed to wander forever and suffer agonies of a man without a home. To assure the corpse all possible safety a low wall of brick was built around the grave and the open space was filled with sand and gravel. In this way a low artificial hill was made which protected the mummy against wild animals and robbers.

Then one day, an Egyptian who had just buried his Mother, of whom he had been particularly fond, decided to give her a monument that should surpass anything that had ever been built in the valley of the Nile.

He gathered his serfs and made them build an artificial mountain that could be seen for miles around. The sides of this hill he covered with a layer of bricks that the sand might not be blown away.

People liked the novelty of the idea.

Soon they were trying to outdo each other and the graves rose twenty and thirty and forty feet above the ground.

At last a rich nobleman ordered a burial chamber made of solid stone.

On top of the actual grave where the mummy rested, he constructed a pile of bricks which rose several hundred feet into the air. A small passage-way gave entrance to the vault and when this passage was closed with a heavy slab of granite the mummy was safe from all intrusion.

The King of course could not allow one of his subjects to outdo him in such a matter. He was the most powerful man of all Egypt who lived in the biggest house and therefore he was entitled to the best grave.

What others had done in brick he could do with the help of more costly materials.

Pharaoh sent his officers far and wide to gather workmen. He constructed roads. He built barracks in which the workmen could live and sleep (you may see those barracks this very day). Then he set to work and made himself a grave which was to endure for all time.

We call this great pile of masonry a "pyramid."

The origin of the word is a curious one.

When the Greeks visited Egypt the Pyramids were already several thousand years old.

THE MUMMY

Of course the Egyptians took their guests into the desert to see these wondrous sights just as we take foreigners to gaze at the Wool-worth Tower and Brooklyn Bridge.

The Greek guest, lost in admiration, waved his hands and asked what the strange mountains might be.

His guide thought that he referred to the extraordinary height and said "Yes, they are very high indeed."

The Egyptian word for height was "pir-em-us."

The Greek must have thought that this was the name of the whole structure and giving it a Greek ending he called it a "pyramis."

We have changed the "s" into a "d" but we still use the same Egyptian word when we talk of the stone graves along the banks of the Nile.

The biggest of these many pyramids, which was built fifty centuries ago, was five hundred feet high.

At the base it was seven hundred and fifty-five feet wide.

It covered more than thirteen acres of desert, which is three times as much space as that occupied by the church of Saint Peter, the largest edifice of the Christian world.

During twenty years, over a hundred thousand men were used to carry the stones from the distant peninsula of Sinai—to ferry them across the Nile (how they ever managed to do this we do not understand)—to drag them halfway across the desert and finally hoist them into their correct position.

But so well did Pharaoh's architects and engineers perform their task that the narrow passage-way which leads to the royal tomb in the heart of the pyramid has never yet been pushed out of shape by the terrific weight of those thousands and thousands of tons of stone which press upon it from all sides.

———————————

THE MAKING OF A STATE

Nowadays we all are members of a "state."

We may be Frenchmen or Chinamen or Russians; we may live in the furthest corner of Indonesia (do you know where that is?), but in some way or other we belong to that curious combination of people which is called the "state."

It does not matter whether we recognize a king or an emperor or a president as our ruler. We are born and we die as a small part of this large Whole and no one can escape this fate.

The "state," as a matter of fact, is quite a recent invention.

The earliest inhabitants of the world did not know what it was.

Every family lived and hunted and worked and died for and by itself. Sometimes it happened that a few of these families, for the sake of greater protection against the wild animals and against other wild people, formed a loose alliance which was called a tribe or a clan. But as soon as the danger was past, these groups of people acted again by and for themselves and if the weak could not defend their own cave, they were left to the mercies of the hyena and the tiger and nobody was very sorry if they were killed.

In short, each person was a nation unto himself and he felt no responsibility for the happiness and safety of his neighbor. Very, very slowly this was changed and Egypt was the first country where the people were organized into a well-regulated empire.

The Nile was directly responsible for this useful development. I have told you how in the summer of each year the greater part of the Nile valley and the Nile delta is turned into a vast inland sea. To derive the greatest benefit from this water and yet survive the flood, it had been necessary at certain points to build dykes and small islands which would offer shelter for man and beast during the months of August and September. The construction of these little artificial islands however had not been simple.

THE YOUNG NILE.

A single man or a single family or even a small tribe could not construct a river-dam without the help of others.

However much a farmer might dislike his neighbors he disliked getting drowned even more and he was obliged to call upon the entire country-side when the water of the river began to rise and threatened him and his wife and his children and his cattle with destruction.

Necessity forced the people to forget their small differences and soon the entire valley of the Nile was covered with little combinations of people who constantly worked together for a common purpose and who depended upon each other for life and prosperity.

Out of such small beginnings grew the first powerful State.

It was a great step forward along the road of progress.

It made the land of Egypt a truly inhabitable place. It meant the end of lawless murder. It assured the people greater safety than ever before and gave the weaker members of the tribe a chance to survive. Nowadays, when conditions of absolute disorder exist only in the jungles of Africa, it is hard to imagine a world without laws and policemen and judges and health officers and hospitals and schools.

But five thousand years ago, Egypt stood alone as an organized state and was greatly envied by those of her neighbors who were obliged to face the difficulties of life single-handedly.

A state, however, is not only composed of citizens.

There must be a few men who execute the laws and who, in case of an emergency, take command of the entire community. Therefore no country has ever been able to endure without a single head, be he called a King or an Emperor or a Shah (as in Persia) or a President, as he is called in our own land.

THE FERTILE VALLEY.

In ancient Egypt, every village recognized the authority of the Village-Elders, who were old men and possessed greater experience than the young ones. These Elders selected a strong man to command their soldiers in case of war and to tell them what to do when there was a flood. They gave him a title which distinguished him from the others. They called him a King or a prince and obeyed his orders for their own common benefit.

Therefore in the oldest days of Egyptian history, we find the following division among the people:

The majority are peasants.

All of them are equally rich and equally poor.

They are ruled by a powerful man who is the commander-in-chief of their armies and who appoints their judges and causes roads to be built for the common benefit and comfort.

He also is the chief of the police force and catches the thieves.

In return for these valuable services he receives a certain amount of everybody's money which is called a tax. The greater part of these taxes, however, do not belong to the King personally. They are money entrusted to him to be used for the common good.

But after a short while a new class of people, neither peasants nor king, begins to develop. This new class, commonly called the nobles, stands between the ruler and his subjects.

Since those early days it has made its appearance in the history of every country and it has played a great role in the development of every nation.

I must try and explain to you how this class of nobles developed out of the most commonplace circumstances of everyday life and why it has maintained itself to this very day, against every form of opposition.

To make my story quite clear, I have drawn a picture.

It shows you five Egyptian farms. The original owners of these farms had moved into Egypt years and years ago. Each had taken a piece of unoccupied land and had settled down upon it to raise grain and cows and pigs and do whatever was necessary to keep themselves and their children alive. Apparently they had the same chance in life.

How then did it happen that one became the ruler of his neighbors and got hold of all their fields and barns without breaking a single law?

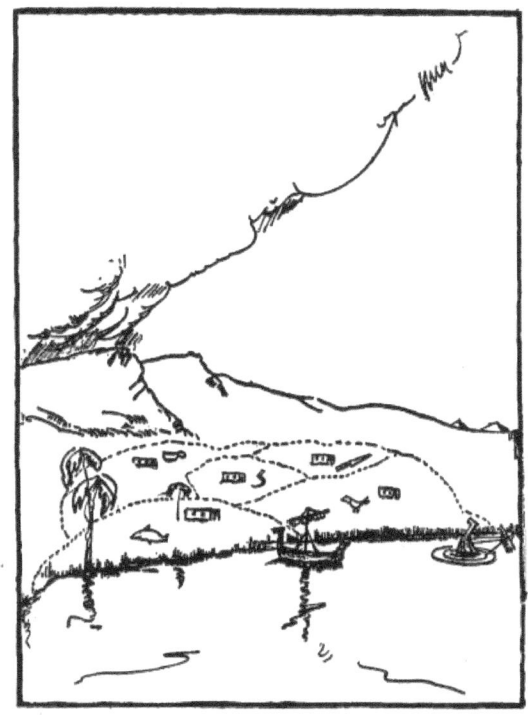

THE ORIGINS OF THE FEUDAL SYSTEM.

One day after the harvest, Mr. Fish (you see his name in hieroglyphics on the map) sent his boat loaded with grain to the town of Memphis to sell the cargo to the inhabitants of central Egypt. It happened to have been a good year for the farmer and Fish got a great deal of money for his wheat. After ten days the boat returned to the homestead and the captain handed the money which he had received to his employer.

A few weeks later, Mr. Sparrow, whose farm was

next to that of Fish, sent his wheat to the nearest market. Poor Sparrow had not been very lucky for the last few years. But he hoped to make up for his recent losses by a profitable sale of his grain. Therefore he had waited until the price of wheat in Memphis should have gone a little higher.

That morning a rumor had reached the village of a famine in the island of Crete. As a result the grain in the Egyptian markets had greatly increased in value.

Sparrow hoped to profit through this unexpected turn of the market and he bade his skipper to hurry.

The skipper handled the rudder of his craft so clumsily that the boat struck a rock and sank, drowning the mate who was caught under the sail.

Sparrow not only lost all his grain and his ship but he was also forced to pay the widow of his drowned mate ten pieces of gold to make up for the loss of her husband.

These disasters occurred at the very moment when Sparrow could not afford another loss.

Winter was near and he had no money to buy cloaks for his children. He had put off buying new hoes and spades for such a long time that the old ones were completely worn out. He had no seeds for his fields. He was in a desperate plight.

He did not like his neighbor, Mr. Fish, any too well but there was no way out. He must go and humbly he must ask for the loan of a small sum of money.

He called on Fish. The latter said that he would

gladly let him have whatever he needed but could Sparrow put up any sort of guaranty?

Sparrow said, "Yes." He would offer his own farm as a pledge of good faith.

Unfortunately Fish knew all about that farm. It had belonged to the Sparrow family for many generations. But the Father of the present owner had allowed himself to be terribly cheated by a Phoenician trader who had sold him a couple of "Phrygian Oxen" (nobody knew what the name meant) which were said to be of a very fine breed, which needed little food and performed twice as much labor as the common Egyptian oxen. The old farmer had believed the solemn words of the impostor. He had bought the wonderful beasts, greatly envied by all his neighbors.

They had not proved a success.

They were very stupid and very slow and exceedingly lazy and within three weeks they had died from a mysterious disease.

The old farmer was so angry that he suffered a stroke and the management of his estate was left to the son, who worked hard but w thout much result.

The loss of his grain and his vessel were the last straw.

Young Sparrow must either starve or ask his neighbor to help him with a loan.

Fish who was familiar with the lives of all his neighbors (he was that kind of person, not because he loved gossip but one never knew how such information might come in handy) and who knew to a penny the state of affairs in the Sparrow household, felt strong enough to insist upon certain terms. Sparrow could have all the money he needed upon the following condition.

He must promise to work for Fish six weeks of every year and he must allow him free access to his grounds at all times.

Sparrow did not like these terms, but the days were growing shorter and winter was coming on fast and his family were without food.

He was forced to accept and from that time on, he and his sons and daughters were no longer quite as free as they had been before.

They did not exactly become the servants or the slaves of their neighbor, but they were dependent upon his kindness for their own livelihood. When they met Fish in the road they stepped aside and said "Good morning, sir." And he answered them—or not—as the case might be.

He now owned a great deal of water-front, twice as much as before.

He had more land and more laborers and he could raise more grain than in the past years. The nearby villagers talked of the new house he was building and in a general way, he was regarded as a man of growing wealth and importance.

Late that summer an unheard-of-thing happened.

It rained.

The oldest inhabitants could not remember such a thing, but it rained hard and steadily for two whole days. A little brook, the existence of which everybody had forgotten, was suddenly turned into a wild torrent. In the middle of the night it came thundering down from the mountains and destroyed the harvest of the farmer who occupied the rocky ground at the foot of the hills. His name was Cup and he too had inherited his land from a hundred other Cups who had gone before. The damage was almost irreparable. Cup needed new seed grain and he needed it at once. He had heard Sparrow's story. He too hated to ask a favor of Fish who was known far and wide as a shrewd dealer. But in the end, he found his way to the Fishs' homestead and humbly begged for the loan of a few bushels of wheat. He got them but not until he had agreed to work two whole months of each year on the farm of Fish.

Fish was now doing very well. His new house was ready and he thought the time had come to establish himself as the head of a household.

Just across the way, there lived a farmer who had a young daughter. The name of this farmer was Knife. He was a happy-go-lucky person and he could not give his child a large dowry.

Fish called on Knife and told him that he did not care for money. He was rich and he was willing to take the daughter without a single penny. Knife, however, must promise to leave his land to his son-in-law in case he died.

This was done.

The will was duly drawn up before a notary, the wedding took place and Fish now possessed (or was about to possess) the greater part of four farms.

It is true there was a fifth farm situated right in between the others. But its owner, by the name of Sickle, could not carry his wheat to the market without crossing the lands over which Fish held sway. Besides, Sickle was not very energetic and he willingly hired himself out to Fish on condition that he and his old wife be given a room and food and clothes for the rest of their days. They had no children and this settlement assured them a peaceful old age.

When Sickle died, a distant nephew appeared who claimed a right to his uncle's farm. Fish had the dogs turned loose on him and the fellow was never seen again.

These transactions had covered a period of twenty years.

The younger generations of the Cup and

Sickle and Sparrow families accepted their situation in life without questioning. They knew old Fish as "the Squire" upon whose good-will they were more or less dependent if they wanted to succeed in life.

When the old man died he left his son many wide acres and a position of great influence among his immediate neighbors.

Young Fish resembled his father. He was very able and had a great deal of ambition. When the king of Upper Egypt went to war against the wild Berber tribes, he volunteered his services.

He fought so bravely that the king appointed him Collector of the Royal Revenue for three hundred villages.

Often it happened that certain farmers could not pay their tax.

Then young Fish offered to give them a small loan.

Before they knew it, they were working for the Royal Tax Gatherer, to repay both the money which they had borrowed and the interest on the loan.

The years went by and the Fish family reigned supreme in the land of their birth. The old home was no longer good enough for such important people.

A noble hall was built (after the pattern of the

Royal Banqueting Hall of Thebes). A high wall was erected to keep the crowd at a respectful distance and Fish never went out without a bodyguard of armed soldiers.

Twice a year he travelled to Thebes to be with his King, who lived in the largest palace of all Egypt and who was therefore known as "Pharaoh," the owner of the "Big House."

Upon one of his visits, he took Fish the Third, grandson of the founder of the family, who was a handsome young fellow.

The daughter of Pharaoh saw the youth and desired him for her husband. The wedding cost Fish most of his fortune, but he was still Collector of the Royal Revenue and by treating the people without mercy he was able to fill his strong-box in less than three years.

When he died he was buried in a small Pyramid, just as if he had been a member of the Royal Family, and a daughter of Pharaoh wept over his grave.

That is my story which begins somewhere along the banks of the Nile and which in the course of three generations lifts a farmer from the ranks of his own humble ancestors and drops him outside the gate but near the throne-room of the King's palace.

What happened to Fish, happened to a large number of equally energetic and resourceful men.

They formed a class apart.

They married each other's daughters and in this way they kept the family fortunes in the hands of a small number of people.

They served the King faithfully as officers in his army and as collectors of his taxes.

They looked after the safety of the roads and the waterways.

They performed many useful tasks and among themselves they obeyed the laws of a very strict code of honor.

If the Kings were bad, the nobles were apt to be bad too.

When the Kings were weak the nobles often managed to get hold of the State.

Then it often happened that the people arose in their wrath and destroyed those who oppressed them.

Many of the old nobles were killed and a new division of the land took place which gave everybody an equal chance.

But after a short while the old story repeated itself.

This time it was perhaps a member of the Sparrow family who used his greater shrewdness and industry to make himself master of the countryside while the descendants of Fish (of glorious memory!) were reduced to poverty.

Otherwise very little was changed.

The faithful peasants continued to work and pay taxes.

The equally faithful tax gatherers continued to gather wealth.

But the old Nile, indifferent to the ambitions of men, flowed as placidly as ever between its age-worn banks and bestowed its fertile blessings upon the poor and upon the rich with the impartial justice which is found only in the forces of nature.

THE RISE AND FALL OF EGYPT

We often hear it said that "civilization travels westward." What we mean is that hardy pioneers have crossed the Atlantic Ocean and settled along the shores of New England and New Netherland—that their children have crossed the vast prairies—that their great-grandchildren have moved into California—and that the present generation hopes to turn the vast Pacific into the most important sea of the ages.

As a matter of fact, "civilization" never remains long in the same spot. It is always going somewhere but it does not always move westward by any means. Sometimes its course points towards the east or the south. Often it zigzags across the map. But it keeps moving. After two or three hundred years, civilization seems to say, "Well, I have been keeping company with these particular people long enough," and it packs its books and its science and its art and its music, and wanders forth in search of new domains. But no one knows whither it is bound, and that is what makes life so interesting.

THE SOIL OF THE FERTILE VALLEY.

In the case of Egypt, the center of civilization moved northward and southward, along the banks of the Nile. First of all, as I told you, people from all over Africa and western Asia moved into the valley and settled down. Thereupon they formed small villages and townships and accepted the rule of a Commander-in-Chief, who was called Pharaoh, and who had his capital in Memphis, in the lower part of Egypt.

After a couple of thousand years, the rulers of this ancient house became too weak to maintain themselves. A new family from the town of Thebes, 350 miles towards the south in Upper Egypt, tried to make itself master of the entire valley. In the year 2400 B.C. they succeeded. As rulers of both Upper and Lower Egypt, they set forth to conquer the rest of the world. They marched towards the sources of the Nile (which they never reached) and conquered black Ethiopia. Next they crossed the desert of Sinai and invaded Syria where they made their name feared by the Babylonians and Assyrians. The possession of these outlying districts assured the safety of Egypt and they could set to work to turn the valley into a happy home, for as many of the people as could find room there. They built many new dikes and dams and a vast reservoir in the desert which they filled with water from the Nile to be kept and used in case of a prolonged drought. They encouraged people to devote themselves to the study of mathematics and astronomy so that they might determine the time when the floods of the Nile were to be expected. Since for this purpose it was necessary to have a handy method by which time could be measured, they established the year of 365 days, which they divided into twelve months.

Contrary to the old tradition which made the Egyptians keep away from all things foreign, they allowed the exchange of Egyptian merchandise for goods which had been carried to their harbors from elsewhere.

They traded with the Greeks of Crete and with the Arabs of western Asia and they got spices from the Indies and they imported gold and silk from China.

But all human institutions are subject to certain definite laws of progress and decline and a State or a dynasty is no exception. After four hundred years of prosperity, these mighty kings showed signs of growing tired. Rather than ride a camel at the head of their army, the rulers of the great

Egyptian Empire stayed within the gates of their palace and listened to the music of the harp or the flute.

One day there came rumors to the town of Thebes that wild tribes of horsemen had been pillaging along the frontiers. An army was sent to drive them away. This army moved into the desert. To the last man it was killed by the fierce Arabs, who now marched towards the Nile, bringing their flocks of sheep and their household goods.

Another army was told to stop their progress. The battle was disastrous for the Egyptians and the valley of the Nile was open to the invaders.

They rode fleet horses and they used bows and arrows. Within a short time they had made themselves master of the entire country. For five centuries they ruled the land of Egypt. They removed the old capital to the Delta of the Nile.

They oppressed the Egyptian peasants.

They treated the men cruelly and they killed the children and they were rude to the ancient gods. They did not like to live in the cities but stayed with their flocks in the open fields and therefore they were called the Hyksos, which means the Shepherd Kings.

At last their rule grew unbearable.

A noble family from the city of Thebes placed itself at the head of a national revolution against the foreign usurpers. It was a desperate fight but the Egyptians won. The Hyksos were driven out of the country, and they went back to the desert whence they had come. The experience had been a warning to the Egyptian people. Their five hundred years of foreign slavery had been a terrible experience. Such a thing must never happen again. The frontier of the fatherland must be made so strong that no one dare to attack the holy soil.

A new Theban king, called Tethmosis, invaded Asia and never stopped until he reached the plains of Mesopotamia. He watered his oxen in the river Euphrates, and Babylon and Nineveh trembled at the mention of his name. Wherever he went, he built strong fortresses, which were connected by excellent roads. Tethmosis, having built a barrier against future invasions, went home and died. But his daughter, Hatshepsut, continued his good work. She rebuilt the temples which the Hyksos had destroyed and she founded a strong state in which soldiers and merchants worked together for a common purpose and which was called the New Empire, and lasted from 1600 to 1300 B.C.

Military nations, however, never last very long. The larger the empire, the more men are needed for its defense and the more men there are in the army, the fewer can stay at home to work the farms and attend to the demands of trade. Within a few years, the Egyptian state had become top-heavy and the army, which was meant to be a bulwark against foreign invasion, dragged the country into ruin from sheer lack of both men and money.

Without interruption, wild people from Asia were attacking those strong walls behind which Egypt was hoarding the riches of the entire civilized world.

At first the Egyptian garrisons could hold their own.

One day, however, in distant Mesopotamia, there arose a new military empire which was called Assyria. It cared for neither art nor science, but it could fight. The Assyrians marched against the Egyptians and defeated them in battle. For more than twenty years they ruled the land of the Nile. To Egypt this meant the beginning of the end.

A few times, for short periods, the people managed to regain their independence. But they were an old race, and they were worn out by centuries of hard work.

The time had come for them to disappear from the stage of history and surrender their leadership as the most civilized people of the world. Greek merchants were swarming down upon the cities at the mouth of the Nile.

A new capital was built at Sais, near the mouth of the Nile, and Egypt became a purely commercial state, the half-way house for the trade between western Asia and eastern Europe.

After the Greeks came the Persians, who conquered all of northern Africa.

Two centuries later, Alexander the Great turned the ancient land of the Pharaoh? into a Greek province. When he died, one of his generals, Ptolemy by name, established himself as the independent king of a new Egyptian state.

The Ptolemy family continued to rule for two hundred years.

In the year 30 B.C., Cleopatra, the last of the Ptolemys, killed herself, rather than become a prisoner of the victorious Roman general, Octavianus.

That was the end.

Egypt became part of the Roman Empire and her life as an independent state ceased for all time.

MESOPOTAMIA, THE COUNTRY BETWEEN THE RIVERS

I am going to take you to the top of the highest pyramid.

It is a good deal of a climb.

The casing of fine stones which in the beginning covered the rough granite blocks which were used to construct this artificial mountain, has long since worn off or has been stolen to help build new Roman cities. A goat would have a fine time scaling this strange peak. But with the help of a few Arab boys, we can get to the top after a few hours of hard work, and there we can rest and look far into the next chapter of the history of the human race.

Way, way off, in the distance, far beyond the yellow sands of the vast desert, through which the old Nile had cut herself a way to the sea, you will (if you have the eyes of a hawk), see something shimmering and green.

It is a valley situated between two big rivers.

It is the most interesting spot of the ancient map.

It is the Paradise of the Old Testament.

It is the old land of mystery and wonder which the Greeks called Mesopotamia.

The word "Mesos" means "middle" or "in between" and "potomos" is the Greek expression for river. (Just think of the Hippopotamus, the horse or "hippos" that lives in the rivers.) Mesopotamia, therefore, meant a stretch of land "between the rivers." The two rivers in this case were the Euphrates which the Babylonians called the "Purattu" and the Tigris, which the

Babylonians called the "Diklat." You will see them both upon the map. They begin their course amidst the snows of the northern mountains of Armenia and slowly they flow through the southern plain until they reach the muddy banks of the Persian Gulf. But before they have lost themselves amidst the waves of this branch of the Indian Ocean, they have performed a great and useful task.

They have turned an otherwise arid and dry region into the only fertile spot of western Asia.

That fact will explain to you why Mesopotamia was so very popular with the inhabitants of the northern mountains and the southern desert.

It is a well-known fact that all living beings like to be comfortable. When it rains, the cat hastens to a place of shelter.

When it is cold, the dog finds a spot in front of the stove. When a certain part of the sea becomes more salty than it has been before (or less, for that matter) myriads of little fishes swim hastily to another part of the wide ocean. As for the birds, a great many of them move from one place to another regularly once a year. When the cold weather sets in, the geese depart, and when the first swallow returns, we know that summer is about to smile upon us.

Man is no exception to this rule. He likes the warm stove much better than the cold wind. Whenever he has the choice between a good dinner and a crust of bread, he prefers the dinner. He will live in the desert or in the snow of the arctic zone if it is absolutely necessary. But offer him a more agreeable place of residence and he will accept without a moment's hesitation. This desire to improve his condition, which really means a desire to make life more comfortable and less wearisome, has been a very good thing for the progress of the world.

It has driven the white people of Europe to the ends of the earth.

It has populated the mountains and the plains of our own country.

It has made many millions of men travel ceaselessly from east to west and from south to north until they have found the climate and the living conditions which suit them best.

In the western part of Asia this instinct which compels living beings to seek the greatest amount of comfort possible with the smallest expenditure of labor forced both the inhabitants of the cold and inhospitable mountains and the people of the parched desert to look for a new dwelling place in the happy valley of Mesopotamia.

It caused them to fight for the sole possession of this Paradise upon Earth.

It forced them to exercise their highest power of inventiveness and their noblest courage to defend their homes and farms and their wives and children against the newcomers, who century after century were attracted by the fame of this pleasant spot.

This constant rivalry was the cause of an everlasting struggle between the old and established tribes and the others who clamored for their share of the soil.

Those who were weak and those who did not have a great deal of energy had little chance of success.

Only the most intelligent and the bravest survived. That will explain to you why Mesopotamia became the home of a strong race of men, capable of creating that state of

civilization which was to be of such enormous
benefit to all later generations.

———————

THE SUMERIAN NAIL WRITERS

In the year 1472, a short time before Columbus discovered America, a certain Venetian, by the name of Josaphat Barbaro, traveling through Persia, crossed the hills near Shiraz and saw something which puzzled him. The hills of Shiraz were covered with old temples which had been cut into the rock of the mountainside. The ancient worshippers had disappeared centuries before and the temples were in a state of great decay. But clearly visible upon their wa ls, Barbara noticed long legends written in a curious script which looked like a series of scratches made by a sharp nail.

When he returned he mentioned his discovery to his fellow-townsmen, but just then the Turks were threatening Europe with an invasion and people were too busy to bother about a new and unknown alphabet, somewhere in the heart of western Asia. The Persian inscriptions therefore were promptly forgotten.

Two and a half centuries later, a noble young Roman by the name of Pietro della Valle visited the same hillsides of Shiraz which Barbaro had passed two hundred years before. He, too, was puzzled by the strange inscriptions on the ruins and being a painstaking young fellow, he copied them carefully and sent his report together with some remarks about the trip to a friend of his, Doctor Schipano, who practiced medicine in Naples and who besides took an interest in matters of learning.

Schipano copied the funny little figures and brought them to the attention of other scientific men. Unfortunately Europe was again occupied with other matters.

The terrible wars between the Protestants and Catholics had broken out and people were busily killing those who disagreed with them upon certain points of a religious nature.

Another century was to pass before the study of the wedge-shaped inscriptions could be taken up seriously.

The eighteenth century—a delightful age for people of an active and curious mind—loved scientific puzzles. Therefore when King Frederick V of Denmark asked for men of learning to join an expedition which he was going to send to western Asia, he found no end of volunteers. His expedition, which left Copenhagen in 1761, lasted six years. During this period all of the members died except one, by the name of Karsten Niebuhr, who had begun life as a German peasant and could stand greater hardships than the professors who had spent their days amidst the stuffy books of their libraries.

This Niebuhr, who was a surveyor by profession, was a young man who deserves our admiration.

He continued his voyage all alone until he reached the ruins of Persepolis where he spent a month copying every inscription that was to be found upon the walls of the ruined palaces and temples.

After his return to Denmark he published his discoveries for the benefit of the scientific world and seriously tried to read some meaning into his own texts.

He was not successful.

But this does not astonish us when we understand the difficulties which he was obliged to solve.

When Champollion tackled the ancient Egyptian

hieroglyphics he was able to make his studies from little pictures.

The writing of Persepolis did not show any pictures at all.

They consisted of v-shaped figures that were repeated endlessly and suggested noth ng at all to the European eye.

Nowadays, when the puzzle has been solved we know that the original script of the Sumerians had been a picture-language, quite as much as that of the Egyptians.

But whereas the Egyptians at a very early date had discovered the papyrus plant and had been able to paint their images upon a smooth surface, the inhabitants of Mesopotamia had been forced to carve their words into the hard rock of a mountain side or into a soft brick of clay.

THE ROCKS OF BEHISTUN.

Driven by necessity they had gradually simplified the original pictures until they devised a system of more than five hundred different letter-combinations which were necessary for their needs.

Let me give you a few examples. In the beginning, a star, when drawn with a nail into a brick looked as follows.

But after a time the star shape was discarded as being too cumbersome and the figure was given this shape. ✸

After a while the meaning of "heaven" was added to that of "star," and the picture was

simplified in this way ⚒ which made t still
more of a puzzle.

In the same way an ox changed from ⬧ into
⚒

A fish changed from ⬧ into ⬧ The sun,

which was originally a plain circle, became ⬧
and if we were using the Sumerian script today

we would make an ⬧ look like this ⬧

You will understand how difficult it was to guess
at the meaning of these figures but the patient
labors of a German schoolmaster by the name of
Grotefend was at last rewarded and thirty years
after the first publication of Niebuhr's texts and
three centuries after the first discovery of the
wedge-formed pictures, four letters had been
deciphered.

These four letters were the D, the A, the R and
the Sh.

They formed the name of Darheush the King,
whom we call Darius.

Then occurred one of those events which were
only possible in those happy days before the
telegraph-wire and the mail-steamer had turned
the entire world into one large city.

While patient European professors were burning
the midnight candles in their attempt to solve
the new Asiatic mystery, young Henry Rawlinson
was serving his time as a cadet of the British
East Indian Company.

He used his spare hours to learn Persian and
when the Shah of Persia asked the English

government for the loan of a few officers to train his native army, Rawlinson was ordered to go to Teheran. He travelled all over Persia and one day he happened to visit the village of Behistun. The Persians called it Bagistana which means the "dwellingplace of the Gods."

Centuries before the main road from Mesopotamia to Iran (the early home of the Persians) had run through this village and the Persian King Darius had used the steep walls of the high cliffs to tell all the world what a great man he was.

High above the roadside he had engraved an account of his glorious deeds.

The inscription had been made in the Persian language, in Babylonian and in the dialect of the city of Susa. To make the story plain to those who could not read at all, a fine piece of sculpture had been added showing the King of Persia placing his triumphant foot upon the body of Gaumata, the usurper who had tried to steal the throne away from the legitimate rulers. For good measure a dozen followers of Gaumata had been added. They stood in the background. Their hands were tied and they were to be executed in a few moments.

The picture and the three texts were several hundred feet above the road but Rawlinson scaled the walls of the rock at great danger to life and limb and copied the entire text.

His discovery was of the greatest importance. The Rock of Behistun became as famous as the Stone of Rosetta and Rawlinson shared the honors of deciphering the old nail-writing with Grotefend.

Although they had never seen each other or heard each other's names, the German schoolmaster and the British officer worked together for a common purpose as all good scientific men should do.

Their copies of the old text were reprinted in every land and by the middle of the nineteenth century, the cuneiform language (so called because the letters were wedge-shaped and "cuneus" is the Latin name for wedge) had given up its secrets. Another human mystery had been solved.

A TOWER OF BABEL.

But about the people who had invented this clever way of writing, we have never been able to learn very much.

They were a white race and they were called the Sumerians.

They lived in a land which we call Shomer and which they themselves called Kengi, which means the "country of the reeds" and which shows us that they had dwelt among the marshy parts of the Mesopotamian valley. Originally the Sumerians had been mountaineers, but the fertile fields had tempted them away from the hills. But while they had left their ancient homes amidst the peaks of western Asia they had not given up their old habits and one of these is of particular interest to us.

Living amidst the peaks of western Asia, they had worshipped their Gods upon altars erected on the tops of rocks. In their new home, among the flat plains, there were no such rocks and it was impossible to construct their shrines in the old fashion. The Sumerians did not like this.

All Asiatic people have a deep respect for tradition and the Sumerian tradition demanded that an altar be plainly visible for miles around.

To overcome this difficulty and keep their peace with the Gods of their Fathers, the Sumerians had built a number of low towers (resembling little hills) on the top of which they had lighted their sacred fires in honor of the old divinities.

When the Jews visited the town of Bab-Illi (which we call Babylon) many centuries after the last of the Sumerians had died, they had been much impressed by the strange-looking towers which stood high amidst the green fields of Mesopotamia. The Tower of Babel of which we hear so much in the Old Testament was nothing but the ruin of an artificial peak, built hundreds of years before by a band of devout Sumerians. It was a curious contraption.

The Sumerians had not known how to construct stairs.

They had surrounded their tower with a sloping gallery which slowly carried people from the bottom to the top.

A few years ago it was found necessary to build a new railroad station in the heart of New York City in such a way that thousands of travelers could be brought from the lower to the higher levels at the same moment.

It was not thought safe to use a staircase for in case of a rush or a panic people might have tumbled and that would have meant a terrible catastrophe.

To solve their problem the engineers borrowed an idea from the Sumerians.

And the Grand Central Station is provided with the same ascending galleries which had first been introduced into the plains of Mesopotamia, three thousand years ago.

ASSYRIA AND BABYLONIA— THE GREAT SEMITIC MELTING-POT

We often call America the "Melting-pot." When we use this term we mean that many races from all over the earth have gathered along the banks of the Atlantic and the Pacific Oceans to find a new home and begin a new career amidst more favorable surroundings than were to be found in the country of their birth. It is true, Mesopotamia was much smaller than our own country. But the fertile valley was the most extraordinary "melting-pot" the world has ever seen and it continued to absorb new tribes for almost two thousand years. The story of each new people, clamoring for homesteads along the banks of the Tigris and the Euphrates is interesting in itself but we can give you only a very short record of their adventures.

HAMMURAPI.

The Sumerians whom we met in the previous chapter, scratching their history upon rocks and bits of clay (and who did not belong to the Semitic race) had been the first nomads to wander into Mesopotamia. Nomads are people who have no settled homes and no grain fields and no vegetable gardens but who live in tents and keep sheep and goats and cows and who move from pasture to pasture, taking their flocks and their tents wherever the grass is green and the water abundant.

Far and wide their mud huts had covered the plains. They were good fighters and for a long time they were able to hold their own against all invaders.

But four thousand years ago a tribe of Semitic desert people called the Akkadians left Arabia, defeated the Sumerians and conquered Mesopotamia. The most famous king of these Akkadians was called Sargon.

He taught his people how to write their own Semitic language in the alphabet of the Sumerians whose territory they had just occupied. He ruled so wisely that soon the differences between the original settlers and the invaders disappeared and they became fast friends and lived together in peace and harmony.

The fame of his empire spread rapidly throughout western Asia and others, hearing of this success, were tempted to try their own luck.

A new tribe of desert nomads, called the Amorites, broke up camp and moved northward.

Thereupon the valley was the scene of a great turmoil until an Amorite chieftain by the name of Hammurapi (or Hammurabi, as you please) established himself in the town of Bab-Illi (which means the Gate of the God) and made himself the ruler of a great Bab-Illian or Babylonian Empire.

This Hammurapi, who lived twenty-one centuries before the birth of Christ, was a very interesting man. He made Babylon the most important town of the ancient world, where learned priests administered the laws which their great Ruler had received from the Sun God himself and where the merchant loved to trade because he was treated fairly and honorably.

Indeed if it were not for the lack of space (these laws of Hammurapi would cover fully forty of these pages if I were to give them to you in detail) I would be able to show you that this ancient Babylonian State was in many respects better managed and that the people were happier and that law and order was maintained more carefully and that there was greater freedom of speech and thought than in many of our modern countries.

But our world was never meant to be too perfect and soon other hordes of rough and murderous men descended from the northern mountains and destroyed the work of Hammurapi's genius.

The name of these new invaders was the Hittites. Of these Hittites I can tell you even less than of the Sumerians. The Bible mentions them. Ruins of their civilization have been found far and wide. They used a strange sort of hieroglyphics but no one has as yet been able to decipher these and read their meaning. They were not greatly gifted as administrators. They ruled only a few years and then their domains fell to pieces.

Of all their glory there remains nothing but a mysterious name and the reputation of having destroyed many things which other people had built up with great pain and care.

Then came another invasion which was of a very different nature.

A fierce tribe of desert wanderers, who murdered and pillaged in the name of their great God Assur, left Arabia and marched northward until they reached the slopes of the mountains. Then they turned eastward and along the banks of the Euphrates they built a city which they called Ninua, a name which has come down to us in the Greek form of Nineveh. At once these new-comers, who are generally known as the Assyrians, began a slow but terrible warfare upon all the other inhabitants of Mesopotamia.

In the twelfth century before Christ they made a first attempt to destroy Babylon but after a first success on the part of their King, Tiglath Pileser, they were defeated and forced to return to their own country.

Five hundred years later they tried again. An adventurous general by the name of Bulu made himself master of the Assyrian throne. He assumed the name of old Tiglath Pileser, who was considered the national hero of the Assyrians and announced his intention of conquering the whole world.

NINEVEH.

He was as good as his word.

Asia Minor and Armenia and Egypt and Northern Arabia and Western Persia and Babylonia became Assyrian provinces. They were ruled by Assyrian governors, who collected the taxes and forced all the young men to serve as soldiers in the Assyrian armies and who made themselves thoroughly hated and despised both for their greed and their cruelty.

Fortunately the Assyrian Empire at its greatest height did not last very long. It was like a ship with too many masts and sails and too small a hull. There were too many soldiers and not enough farmers—too many generals and not enough business men.

The King and the nobles grew very rich but the masses lived in squalor and poverty. Never for a moment was the country at peace. It was for ever fighting someone, somewhere, for causes which did not interest the subjects at all. Until, through this continuous and exhausting warfare, most of the Assyrian soldiers had been killed or maimed and it became necessary to allow foreigners to enter the army. These foreigners had little love for their brutal masters who had destroyed their homes and had stolen their children and therefore they fought badly.

Life along the Assyrian frontier was no longer safe.

Strange new tribes were constantly attacking the northern boundaries. One of these was called the Cimmerians. The Cimmerians, when we first hear of them, inhabited the vast plain beyond the northern mountains. Homer describes their country in his account of the voyage of Odysseus and he tells us that it was a place "for ever steeped in darkness." They were a race of white men and they had been driven out of their former homes by still another group of Asiatic wanderers, the Scythians.

The Scythians were the ancestors of the modern Cossacks, and even in those remote days they were famous for their horsemanship.

NINEVEH DESTROYED.

The Cimmerians, hard pressed by the Scythians, crossed from Europe into Asia and conquered the land of the Hittites. Then they left the mountains of Asia Minor and descended into the valley of Mesopotamia, where they wrought terrible havoc among the impoverished people of the Assyrian Empire.

Nineveh called for volunteers to stop this invasion. Her worn-out regiments marched northward when news came of a more immediate and formidable danger.

For many years a small tribe of Semitic nomads, called the Chaldeans, had been living peacefully in the south-eastern part of the fertile valley, in the country called Ur. Suddenly these Chaldeans had gone upon the war-path and had begun a regular campaign against the Assyrians.

Attacked from all sides, the Assyrian State, which had never gained the good-will of a single neighbor, was doomed to perish.

When Nineveh fell and this forbidding treasure house, filled with the plunder of centuries, was at last destroyed, there was joy in every hut and hamlet from the Persian Gulf to the Nile.

And when the Greeks visited the Euphrates a few generations later and asked what these vast ruins, covered with shrubs and trees might be, there was no one to tell them.

The people had hastened to forget the very name of the city that had been such a cruel master and had so miserably oppressed them.

Babylon, on the other hand, which had ruled its subjects in a very different way, came back to life.

During the long reign of the wise King Nebuchadnezzar the ancient temples were rebuilt. Vast palaces were erected within a short space of time. New canals were dug all over the valley to help irrigate the fields. Quarrelsome neighbors were severely punished.

Egypt was reduced to a mere frontier-province and Jerusalem, the capital of the Jews, was destroyed. The Holy Books of Moses were taken to Babylon and several thousand Jews were forced to follow the Babylonian King to his capital as hostages for the good behavior of those who remained behind in Palestine.

But Babylon was made into one of the seven wonders of the ancient world.

Trees were planted along the banks of the Euphrates.

Flowers were made to grow upon the many walls of the city and after a few years it seemed that a thousand gardens were hanging from the roofs of the ancient town.

As soon as the Chaldeans had made their capital the show-place of the world they devoted their attention to matters of the mind and of the spirit.

Like all desert folk they were deeply interested in the stars which at night had guided them safely through the trackless desert.

They studied the heavens and named the twelve signs of the Zodiak.

They made maps of the sky and they discovered the first five planets. To these they gave the names of their Gods. When the Romans conquered Mesopotamia they translated the Chaldean names into Latin and that explains why today we talk of Jupiter and Venus and Mars and Mercury and Saturn.

They divided the equator into three hundred and sixty degrees and they divided the day into twenty-four hours and the hour into sixty minutes and no modern man has ever been able to improve upon this old Babylonian invention. They possessed no watches but they measured time by the shadow of the sun-dial.

They learned to use both the decimal and the duodecimal systems (nowadays we use only the decimal system, which is a great pity). The duodecimal system (ask your father what the word means), accounts for the sixty minutes and the sixty seconds and the twenty-four hours which seem to have so little in common with our modern world which would have divided day and night into twenty hours and the hour into fifty minutes and the minute into fifty seconds according to the rules of the restricted decimal system.

The Chaldeans also were the first people to recognize the necessity of a regular day of rest.

When they divided the year into weeks they ordered that six days of labor should be followed by one day, devoted to the "peace of the soul."

THE CHALDEANS.

It was a great pity that the center of so much intelligence and industry could not exist forever. But not even the genius of a number of very wise Kings could save the ancient people of Mesopotamia from their ultimate fate.

The Semitic world was growing old.

It was time for a new race of men.

In the fifth century before Christ, an Indo-European people called the Persians (I shall tell you about them later) left its pastures amidst the high mountains of Iran and conquered the fertile valley.

The city of Babylon was captured without a struggle.

Nabonidus, the last Babylonian king, who had been more interested in religious problems than in defending his own country, fled.

A few days later his small son, who had remained behind, died.

Cyrus, the Persian King, buried the child with great honor and then proclaimed himself the legitimate successor of the old rulers of Babylonia.

Mesopotamia ceased to be an independent State.

It became a Persian province ruled by a Persian "Satrap" or Governor.

As for Babylon, when the Kings no longer used the city as their residence it soon lost all importance and became a mere country village.

In the fourth century before Christ it enjoyed another spell of glory.

It was in the year 331 B.C. that Alexander the Great, the young Greek who had just conquered Persia and India and Egypt and every other place, visited the ancient city of sacred memories. He wanted to use the old city as a background for his own newly-acquired glory. He began to rebuild the palace and ordered that the rubbish be removed from the temples.

Unfortunately he died quite suddenly in the Banqueting Hall of Nebuchadnezzar and after that nothing on earth could save Babylon from her ruin.

As soon as one of Alexander's generals, Seleucus Nicator, had perfected the plans for a new city at the mouth of the great canal which united the Tigris and the Euphrates, the fate of Babylon was sealed.

A tablet of the year 275 B.C. tells us how the last of the Babylonians were forced to leave their home and move into this new settlement which had been called Seleucia.

Even then, a few of the faithful continued to visit the holy places which were now inhabited by wolves and jackals.

The majority of the people, little interested in those half-forgotten divinities of a bygone age, made a more practical use of their former home.

They used it as a stone-quarry.

For almost thirty centuries Babylon had been the great spiritual and intellectual center of the Semitic world and a hundred generations had regarded the city as the most perfect expression of their people's genius.

It was the Paris and London and New York of the ancient world.

At present three large mounds show us where the ruins lie buried beneath the sand of the ever-encroaching desert.

THIS IS THE STORY OF MOSES

High above the thin line of the distant horizon there appeared a small cloud of dust. The Babylonian peasant, working his poor farm on the outskirts of the fertile lands, noticed it.

"Another tribe is trying to break into our land," he said to himself. "They will not get far. The King's soldiers will drive them away."

He was right. The frontier guards welcomed the new arrivals with drawn swords and bade them try their luck elsewhere.

They moved westward following the borders of the land of Babylon and they wandered until they reached the shores of the Mediterranean.

There they settled down and tended their flocks and lived the simple lives of their earliest ancestors who had dwelt in the land of Ur.

Then there came a time when the rain ceased to fall and there was not enough to eat for man or beast and it became necessary to look for new pastures or perish on the spot.

Once more the shepherds (who were called the Hebrews) moved their families into a new home which they found along the banks of the Red Sea near the land of Egypt.

But hunger and want had followed them upon their voyage and they were forced to go to the Egyptian officials and beg for food that they might not starve.

The Egyptians had long expected a famine. They had built large store-houses and these were all filled with the surplus wheat of the last seven years. This wheat was now being distributed among the people and a food-dictator had been appointed to deal it out equally to the rich and to the poor. His name was Joseph and he belonged to the tribe of the Hebrews.

As a mere boy he had run away from his own family. It was said that he had escaped to save himself from the anger of his brethren who envied him because he was the favorite of their Father.

Whatever the truth, Joseph had gone to Egypt and he had found favor in the eyes of the Hyksos Kings who had just conquered the country and who used this bright young man to assist them in administering their new possessions.

As soon as the hungry Hebrews appeared before Joseph with their request for help, Joseph recognized his relatives.

But he was a generous man and all meanness of spirit was foreign to his soul.

He did not revenge himself upon those who had wronged him but he gave them wheat and allowed them to settle in the land of Egypt, they and their children and their flocks—and be happy.

For many years the Hebrews (who are more commonly known as the Jews) lived in the eastern part of their adopted country and all was well with them.

Then a great change took place.

A sudden revolution deprived the Hyksos Kings of their power and forced them to leave the country. Once more the Egyptians were masters within their own house. They had never liked foreigners any too well. Three hundred years of oppression by a band of Arab shepherds had greatly increased this feeling of loathing for everything that was alien.

MOSES.

The Jews on the other hand had been onfriendly terms with the Hyksos who were related to them by blood and by race. This was enough to make them traitors in the eyes of the Egyptians.

Joseph no longer lived to protect his people.

After a short struggle they were taken away from their old homes, they were driven into the heart of the country and they were treated like slaves.

For many years they performed the dreary tasks of common laborers, carrying stones for the building of pyramids, making bricks for public buildings, constructing roads, and digging canals to carry the water of the Nile to the distant Egyptian farms.

Their suffering was great but they never lost courage and help was near.

There lived a certain young man whose name was Moses. He was very intelligent anc he had received a good education because the Egyptians had decided that he should enter the service of Pharaoh.

If nothing had happened to arouse his anger, Moses would have ended his days peacefully as the governor of a small province or the collector of taxes of an outlying district.

But the Egyptians, as I have told you before, despised those who did not look like themselves nor dress in true Egyptian fashion and they were apt to insult such people because they were "different."

And because the foreigners were in the minority they could not well defend themselves. Nor did it serve any good purpose to carry their complaints before a tribunal for the Judge did not smile upon the grievances of a man who refused to worship the Egyptian gods and who pleaded his case with a strong foreign accent.

Now it occurred one day that Moses was taking a walk with a few of his Egyptian friends and one of these said something particularly disagreeable about the Jews and even threatened to lay hands on them.

Moses, who was a hot-headed youth hit him.

The blow was a bit too severe and the Egyptian fell down dead.

To kill a native was a terrible thing and the Egyptian laws were not as wise as those of Hammurapi, the good Babylonian King, who recognized the difference between a premeditated murder and the killing of a man whose insults had brought his opponent to a point of unreasoning rage.

Moses fled.

He escaped into the land of his ancestors, into the Midian desert, along the eastern bank of the Red Sea, where his tribe had tended their sheep several hundred years before.

A kind priest by the name of Jethro received him in his house and gave him one of his seven daughters, Zipporah, as his wife.

There Moses lived for a long time and there he pondered upon many deep subjects. He had left the luxury and the comfort of the palace of Pharaoh to share the rough and simple life of a desert priest.

In the olden days, before the Jewish people had moved into Egypt, they too had been wanderers among the endless plains of Arabia. They had lived in tents and they had eaten plain food, but they had been honest men and faithful women, contented with few possessions but proud of the righteousness of their mind.

All this had been changed after they had become exposed to the civilization of Egypt. They had taken to the ways of the comfort-loving Egyptians. They had allowed another race to rule them and they had not cared to fight for their independence.

Instead of the old gods of the wind-swept desert they had begun to worship strange divinities who lived in the glimmering splendors of the dark Egyptian temples.

Moses felt that it was his duty to go forth and save his people from their fate and bring them back to the simple Truth of the olden days.

And so he sent messengers to his relatives and suggested that they leave the land of slavery and join him in the desert.

But the Egyptians heard of this and guarded the Jews more carefully than ever before.

It seemed that the plans of Moses were doomed to failure when suddenly an epidemic broke out among the people of the Nile Valley.

The Jews who had always obeyed certain very strict laws of health (which they had learned in the hardy days of their desert life) escaped the disease while the weaker Egyptians died by the hundreds of thousands.

Amidst the confusion and the panic which followed this Silent Death, the Jews packed their belongings and hastily fled from the land which had promised them so much and which had given them so little.

As soon as the flight became known the Egyptians tried to follow them with their armies but their soldiers met with disaster and the Jews escaped.

They were safe and they were free and they moved eastward into the waste spaces which are situated at the foot of Mount Sinai, the peak which has been called after Sin, the Babylonian God of the Moon.

There Moses took command of his fellow-tribesmen and commenced upon his great task of reform.

In those days, the Jews, like all other people, worshipped many gods. During their stay in Egypt they had even learned to do homage to those animals which the Egyptians held in such high honor that they built holy shrines for their special benefit. Moses on the other hand, during his long and lonely life amidst the sandy hills of the peninsula, had learned to revere the strength and the power of the great God of the

Storm and the Thunder, who ruled the high heavens and upon whose good-will the wanderer in the desert depended for life and light and breath.

This God was called Jehovah and he was a mighty Being who was held in trembling respect by all the Semitic people of western Asia.

Through the teaching of Moses he was to become the sole Master of the Jewish race.

One day Moses disappeared from the camp of the Hebrews. He took with him two tablets of rough-hewn stone. It was whispered that he had gone to seek the solitude of Mount Sinai's highest peak.

That afternoon, the top of the mountain was lost to sight.

The darkness of a terrible storm hid it from the eye of man.

But when Moses returned, behold! … there stood engraved upon the tablets the words which Jehovah himself had spoken amidst the crash of his thunder and the blinding flashes of his lightning.

From that moment on, no Jew dared to question the authority of Moses.

When he told his people that Jehovah commanded them to continue their wanderings, they obeyed with eagerness.

For many years they lived amidst the trackless hills of the desert.

They suffered great hardships and almost perished from lack of food and water.

But Moses kept high their hopes of a Promised Land which would offer a lasting home to the true followers of Jehovah.

At last they reached a more fertile region.

They crossed the river Jordan and, carrying the Holy Tablets of Law, they made ready to occupy the pastures which stretch from Dan to Beersheba.

As for Moses, he was no longer their leader.

He had grown old and he was very tired.

He had been allowed to see the distant ridges of the Palestine Mountains among which the Jews were to find a Fatherland.

Then he had closed his wise eyes for all time.

He had accomplished the task which he had set himself in his youth.

He had led his people out of foreign slavery into the new freedom of an independent life.

He had united them and he had made them the first of all nations to worship a single God.

JERUSALEM—THE CITY OF THE LAW

Palestine is a small strip of land between the mountains of Syria and the green waters of the Mediterranean. It has been inhabited since time immemorial, but we do not know very much about the first settlers, although we have given them the name of Canaanites.

The Canaanites belonged to the Semitic race. Their ancestors, like those of the Jews and the Babylonians, had been a desert folk. But when the Jews entered Palestine, the Canaanites lived in towns and villages. They were no longer shepherds but traders. Indeed, in the Jewish language, Canaanite and merchant came to mean the same thing.

They had built themselves strong cities, surrounded by high walls and they did not allow the Jews to enter their gates, but they forced them to keep to the open country and make their home amidst the grassy lands of the valleys.

After a time, however, the Jews and the Canaanites became friends. This was not so very difficult for they both belonged to the same race. Besides they feared a common enemy and only their united strength could defend their country against these dangerous neighbors, who were called the Philistines and who belonged to an entirely different race.

The Philistines really had no business in Asia. They were Europeans, and their earliest home had been in the Isle of Crete. At what age they had settled along the shores of the Mediterranean is quite uncertain because we do not know when the Indo-European invaders had driven them from their island home. But even the Egyptians, who called them Purasati, had feared them greatly and when the Philistines (who wore a headdress of feathers just like our Indians) went upon the war-path, all the people of western Asia sent large armies to protect their frontiers.

JERUSALEM.

As for the war between the Philistines and the Jews, it never came to an end. For although David slew Goliath (who wore a suit of armor which was a great curiosity in those days and had been no doubt imported from the island of Cyprus where the copper mines of the ancient world were found) and although Samson killed the Philistines wholesale when he buried himself and his enemies beneath the temple of Dagon, the Philistines always proved themselves more than a match for the Jews and never allowed the Hebrew people to get hold of any of the harbors of the Mediterranean.

The Jews therefore were obliged by fate to content themselves with the valleys of eastern Palestine and there, on the top of a barren hill, they erected their capital.

The name of this city was Jerusalem and for thirty centuries it has been one of the most holy spots of the western world.

In the dim ages of the unknown past, Jerusalem, the Home of Peace, had been a little fortified outpost of the Egyptians who had built many small fortifications and castles along the mountain ridges of Palestine, to defend their outlying frontier against attacks from the East.

After the downfall of the Egyptian Empire, a native tribe, the Jebusites, had moved into the deserted city. Then came the Jews who captured the town after a long struggle and made it the residence of their King David.

At last, after many years of wandering the Tables of the Law seemed to have reached a place of enduring rest. Solomon, the Wise, decided to provide them with a magnificent home. Far and wide his messengers travelled to ransack the world for rare woods and precious metals. The entire nation was asked to offer its wealth to make the House of God worthy of its holy name. Higher and higher the walls of the temple arose guarding the sacred Laws of Jehovah for all the ages.

Alas, the expected eternity proved to be of short duration. Themselves intruders among hostile neighbors, surrounded by enemies on all sides, harassed by the Philistines, the Jews did not maintain their independence for very long.

They fought well and bravely. But their little state, weakened by petty jealousies, was easily overpowered by the Assyrians and the Egyptians and the Chaldeans and when Nebuchadnezzar, the King of Babylon, took Jerusalem in the year 586 before the birth of Christ, he destroyed the city and the temple, and the Tablets of Stone went up in the general conflagration.

At once the Jews set to work to rebuild their holy shrine. But the days of Solomon's glory were gone. The Jews were the subjects of a foreign race and money was scarce. It took seventy years to reconstruct the old edifice. It stood securely for three hundred years but then a second invasion took place and once more the red flames of the burning temple brightened the skies of Palestine.

When it was rebuilt for the third time, it was surrounded by two high walls with narrow gates and several inner courts were added to make sudden invasion in the future an impossibility.

But ill-luck pursued the city of Jerusalem.

In the sixty-fifth year before the birth of Christ, the Romans under their general Pompey took possession of the Jewish capital. Their practical sense did not take kindly to an old city with crooked and dark streets and many unhealthy alley-ways. They cleaned up this old rubbish (as they considered it) and built new barracks and large public buildings and swimming-pools and athletic parks and they forced their modern improvements upon an unwilling populace.

The temple which served no practical purposes (as far as they could see) was neglected until the days of Herod, who was King of the Jews by the Grace of the Roman sword and whose vanity wished to renew the ancient splendor of the bygone ages. In a half-hearted manner the oppressed people set to work to obey the orders of a master who was not of their own choosing.

When the last stone had been placed in its proper position another revolution broke out against the merciless Roman tax gatherers. The temple was the first victim of this rioting. The soldiers of the Emperor Titus promptly set fire to this center of the old Jewish faith. But the city of Jerusalem was spared.

Palestine however continued to be the scene of unrest.

The Romans who were familiar with all sorts of races of men and who ruled countries where a thousand different divinities were worshipped did not know how to handle the Jews. They did not understand the Jewish character at all. Extreme tolerance (based upon indifference) was the foundation upon which Rome had constructed her very successful Empire. Roman governors never interfered with the religious belief of subject tribes. They demanded that a picture or a statue of the Emperor be placed in the temples of the people who inhabited the outlying parts of the Roman domains. This was a mere formality and it did not have any deep significance. But to the Jews such a thing seemed highly sacrilegious and they would not desecrate their Holiest of Holies by the carven image of a Roman potentate.

They refused.

The Romans insisted.

In itself a matter of small importance, a misunderstanding of this sort was bound to grow and cause further ill-feeling. Fifty-two years after the revolt under the Emperor Titus the Jews once more rebelled. This time the Romans decided to be thorough in their work of destruction.

Jerusalem was destroyed.

The temple was burned down.

A new Roman city, called Aelia Capitolina was erected upon the ruins of the old city of Solomon.

A heathenish temple devoted to the worship of Jupiter was built upon the site where the faithful had worshipped Jehovah for almost a thousand years.

The Jews themselves were expelled from their capital and thousands of them were driven away from the home of their ancestors.

From that moment on they became wanderers upon the face of the Earth.

But the Holy Laws no longer needed the safe shelter of a royal shrine.

Their influence had long since passed beyond the narrow confines of the land of Judah. They had become a living symbol of Justice wherever honorable people tried to live a rightecus life.

DAMASCUS—THE CITY OF TRADE

The old cities of Egypt have disappeared from the face of the earth. Nineveh and Babylon are deserted mounds of dust and brick. The ancient temple of Jerusalem lies buried beneath the blackened ruins of its own glory.

One city alone has survived the ages.

It is called Damascus.

Within its four great gates and its strong walls a busy people has followed its daily occupations for five thousand consecutive years and the "Street called Straight" which is the city's main artery of commerce, has seen the coming and going of one hundred and fifty generations.

Humbly Damascus began its career as a fortified frontier town of the Amorites, those famous desert folk who had given birth to the great King Hammurapi. When the Amorites moved further eastward into the valley of Mesopotamia to found the Kingdom of Babylon, Damascus had been continued as a trading post with the wild Hittites who inhabited the mountains of Asia Minor.

In due course of time the earliest inhabitants had been absorbed by another Semitic tribe, called the Aramaeans. The city itself however had not changed its character. It remained throughout these many changes an important center of commerce.

It was situated upon the main road from Egypt to Mesopotamia and it was within a week's distance from the harbors on the Mediterranean. It produced no great generals and statesmen and no famous Kings. It did not conquer a single mile of neighboring territory. It traded with all the world and offered a safe home to the merchant and to the artisan. Incidentally it bestowed its language upon the greater part of western Asia.

Commerce has always demanded quick and practical ways of communication between different nations. The elaborate system of nail-writing of the ancient Sumerians was too involved for the Aramaean business man. He invented a new alphabet which could be written much faster than the old wedge-shaped figures of Babylon.

The spoken language of the Aramaeans followed their business correspondence.

Aramaean became the English of the ancient world. In most parts of Mesopotamia it was understood as readily as the native torgue. In some countries it actually took the place of the old tribal dialect.

And when Christ preached to the multitudes, he did not use the ancient Jewish speech in which Moses had explained the Laws unto his fellow wanderers.

He spoke in Aramaean, the language of the merchant, which had become the language of the simple people of the old Mediterranean world.

THE PHOENICIANS WHO SAILED BEYOND THE HORIZON

A pioneer is a brave fellow, with the courage of his own curiosity.

Perhaps he lives at the foot of a high mountain.

So do thousands of other people. They are quite contented to leave the mountain alone.

But the pioneer feels unhappy. He wants to know what mysteries this mountain hides from his eyes. Is there another mountain behind it, or a plain? Does it suddenly arise with its steep cliffs from the dark waves of the ocean or does it overlook a desert?

One fine day the true pioneer leaves his family and the safe comfort of his home to go and find out. Perhaps he will come back and tell his experience to his indifferent relatives. Or he will be killed by falling stones or a treacherous blizzard. In that case he does not return at all and the good neighbors shake their heads and say, "He got what he deserved. Why did he not stay at home like the rest of us?"

THE DISTANT HORIZON

But the world needs such men and after they have been dead for many years and others have reaped the benefits of their discoveries, they always receive a statue with a fitting inscription.

More terrifying than the highest mountain is the thin line of the distant horizon. It seems to be the end of the world itself. Heaven have mercy upon those who pass beyond this meeting-place of sky and water, where all is black despair and death.

And for centuries and centuries after man had built his first clumsy boats, he remained within the pleasant sight of one familiar shore and kept away from the horizon.

Then came the Phoenicians who knew no such

117

fears. They passed beyond the sight of land. Suddenly the forbidding ocean was turned into a peaceful highway of commerce and the dangerous menace of the horizon became a myth.

These Phoenician navigators were Semites. Their ancestors had lived in the desert of Arabia together with the Babylonians, the Jews and all the others. But when the Jews occupied Palestine, the cities of the Phoenicians were already old with the age of many centuries.

There were two Phoenician centers of trade.

One was called Tyre and the other was called Sidon. They were built upon high cliffs and rumor had it that no enemy could take them. Far and wide their ships sailed to gather the products of the Mediterranean for the benefit of the people of Mesopotamia.

At first the sailors only visited the distant shores of France and Spain to barter with the natives and hastened home with their grain and metal. Later they had built fortified trading posts along the coasts of Spain and Italy and Greece and the far-off Scilly Islands where the valuable tin was found.

THE PHOENICIANS.

To the uncivilized savages of Europe, such a trading post appeared as a dream of beauty and luxury. They asked to be allowed to live close to its walls, to see the wonderful sights when the boats of many sails entered the harbor, carrying the much-desired merchandise of the unknown east. Gradually they left their huts to build themselves small wooden houses around the Phoenician fortresses. In this way many a trading post had grown into a market place for all the people of the entire neighborhood.

Today such big cities as Marseilles and Cadiz are proud of their Phoenician origin, but their ancient mothers, Tyre and Sidon, have been dead and forgotten for over two thousand years and of the Phoenicians themselves, none have survived.

This is a sad fate but it was fully deserved.

The Phoenicians had grown rich without great effort, but they had not known how to use their wealth wisely. They had never cared for books or learning. They had only cared for money.

They had bought and sold slaves all over the world. They had forced the foreign immigrants to work in their factories. They cheated their neighbors whenever they had a chance and they had made themselves detested by all the other people of the Mediterranean.

They were brave and energetic navigators, but they showed themselves cowards whenever they were obliged to choose between honorable dealing and an immediate profit, obtained through fraudulent and shrewd trading.

As long as they had been the only sailors in the world who could handle large ships, all other nations had been in need of their services. As soon as the others too had learned how to handle a rudder and a set of sails, they at once got rid of the tricky Phoenician merchant.

From that moment on, Tyre and Sidon had lost their old hold upon the commercial world of Asia. They had never encouraged art or science. They had known how to explore the seven seas and turn their ventures into profitable investments. No state, however, can be safely built upon material possessions alone.

The land of Phoenicia had always been a counting-house without a soul.

It perished because it had honored a well-filled

treasure chest as the highest ideal of c vic pride.

———————————

THE ALPHABET FOLLOWS THE TRADE

I have told you how the Egyptians preserved speech by means of little figures. I have described the wedge-shaped signs which served the people of Mesopotamia as a handy means of transacting business at home and abroad.

But how about our own alphabet? From whence came those compact little letters which follow us throughout our life, from the date on our birth certificate to the last word of our funeral notice? Are they Egyptian or Babylonian or Aramaic or are they something entirely different? They are a little bit of everything, as I shall now tell you.

Our modern alphabet is not a very satisfactory instrument for the purpose of reproducing our speech. Some day a genius will invent a new system of writing which shall give each one of our sounds a little picture of its own. But with all its many imperfections the letters of our modern alphabet perform their daily task quite nicely and fully as well as their very accurate and precise cousins, the numerals, who wandered into Europe from distant India, almost ten centuries after the first invasion of the alphabet. The earliest history of these letters, however, is a deep mystery and it will take many years of painstaking investigation before we can solve it.

This much we know—that our alphabet was not suddenly invented by a bright young scribe. It developed and grew during hundreds of years out of a number of older and more complicated systems.

In my last chapter I have told you of the language of the intelligent Aramaean traders which spread throughout western Asia, as an international means of communication. The language of the Phoenicians was never very popular among their neighbors. Except for a very few words we do not know what sort of tongue it was. Their system of writing, however, was carried into every corner of the vast Mediterranean and every Phoenician colony became a center for its further distribution.

It remains to be explained why the Phoenicians, who did nothing to further either art or science, hit upon such a compact and handy system of writing, while other and superior nations remained faithful to the old clumsy scribbling.

The Phoenicians, before all else, were practical business men. They did not travel abroad to admire the scenery. They went upon their perilous voyages to distant parts of Europe and more distant parts of Africa in search of wealth. Time was money in Tyre and Sidon and commercial documents written in hieroglyphics or Sumerian wasted useful hours of busy clerks who might be employed upon more useful errands.

When our modern business world decided that the old-fashioned way of dictating letters was too slow for the hurry of modern life, a clever man devised a simple system of dots and dashes which could follow the spoken word as closely as a hound follows a hare.

This system we call "shorthand."

The Phoenician traders did the same thing.

They borrowed a few pictures from the Egyptian hieroglyphics and simplified a number of wedge-shaped figures from the Babylonians.

They sacrificed the pretty looks of the older system for the benefit of speed and they reduced the thousands of images of the ancient world to a short and handy alphabet of only twenty-two letters. They tried it out at home and when it proved a success, they carried it abroad.

Among the Egyptians and the Babylonians, writing had been a very serious affair—something almost holy. Many improvements had been proposed but these had been invariably discarded as sacrilegious innovations. The Phoenicians who were not interested in piety succeeded where the others had failed. They could not introduce their script into Mesopotamia and Egypt, but among the people of the Mediterranean, who were totally ignorant of the art of writing, the Phoenician alphabet was a great success and in all nooks and corners of that vast sea we find vases and pillars and ruins covered with Phoenician inscriptions.

The Indo-European Greeks who had migrated to the many islands of the Aegean Sea at once applied this foreign alphabet to their own language. Certain Greek sounds, unknown to the ears of the Semitic Phoenicians, needed letters of their own. These were invented and added to the others.

But the Greeks did not stop at this.

They improved the whole system of speech-recording.

All the systems of writing of the ancient people of Asia had one thing in common.

The consonants were reproduced but the reader was forced to guess at the vowels.

This is not as difficult as it seems.

We often omit the vowels in advertisements and in announcements which are printed in our newspapers. Journalists and telegraph operators, too, are apt to invent languages of their own which do away with all the superfluous vowels and use only such consonants as are necessary to provide a skeleton around which the vowels can be draped when the story is rewritten.

But such an imperfect scheme of writing can never become popular, and the Greeks, with their sense of order, added a number of extra signs to reproduce the "a" and the "e" and the "i" and the "o" and the "u." When this had been done, they possessed an alphabet which allowed them to write everything in almost every language.

Five centuries before the birth of Christ these letters crossed the Adriatic and wandered from Athens to Rome.

The Roman soldiers carried them to the furthest corners of western Europe and taught our own ancestors the use of the little Phoenician signs.

Twelve centuries later, the missionaries of Byzantine took the alphabet into the dreary wilderness of the dark Russian plain.

Today more than half of the people of the world use this Asiatic alphabet to keep a record of their thoughts and to preserve a record of their knowledge for the benefit of their children and their grandchildren.

THE END OF THE ANCIENT WORLD

So far, the story of ancient man has been the record of a wonderful achievement. Along the banks of the river Nile, in Mesopotamia and on the shores of the Mediterranean, people had accomplished great things and wise rulers had performed mighty deeds. There, for the first time in history, man had ceased to be a roving animal. He had built himself houses and villages and vast cities.

He had formed states.

He had learned the art of constructing and navigating swift-sailing boats.

He had explored the heavens and within his own soul he had discovered certain great moral laws which made him akin to the divinities which he worshipped. He had laid the foundations for all our further knowledge and our science and our art and those things that tend to make life sublime beyond the mere grubbing for food and lodging.

Most important of all he had devised a system of recording sound which gave unto his children and unto his children's children the benefit of their ancestors' experience and allowed them to accumulate such a store of information that they could make themselves the masters of the forces of nature.

But together with these many virtues, ancient man had one great failing.

He was too much a slave of tradition.

He did not ask enough questions.

He reasoned "My father did such and such a

126

thing before me and my grandfather did it before my father and they both fared well and therefore this thing ought to be good for me too and I must not change it." He forgot that this patient acceptance of facts would never have lifted us above the common herd of animals.

Once upon a time there must have been a man of genius who refused any longer to swing from tree to tree with the help of his long, curly tail (as all his people had done before him) and who began to walk on his feet.

But ancient man had lost sight of this fact and continued to use the wooden plow of h s earliest ancestors and continued to believe in the same gods that had been worshipped ten thousand years before and taught his children to do likewise.

Instead of going forward he stood still and this was fatal.

For a new and more energetic race appeared upon the horizon and the ancient world was doomed.

We call these new people the Indo-Europeans. They were white men like you and me, and they spoke a language which was the common ancestor of all our European languages with the exception of Hungarian, Finnish and the Basque of Northern Spain.

When we first hear of them they had for many centuries made their home along the banks of the Caspian Sea. But one day (for reasons which are totally unknown to us) they packed their belongings on the backs of the horses which they had trained and they gathered their cows and dogs and goats and began to wander in search of distant happiness and food. Some of them moved into the mountains of central Asia and for a long time they lived amidst the peaks of the plateau of Iran, whence they are called the Iranians or Aryans. Others slowly followed the setting sun and took possession of the vast plains of western Europe.

A COLONY.

They were almost as uncivilized as those prehistoric men who made their appearance within the first pages of this book. But they were a hardy race and good fighters and without difficulty they seem to have occupied the hunting grounds and the pastures of the men of the stone age.

They were as yet quite ignorant but thanks to a happy Fate they were curious. The wisdom of the ancient world, which was carried to them by the traders of the Mediterranean, they very soon made their own.

But the age-old learning of Egypt and Babylonia and Chaldea they merely used as a stepping-stone to something higher and better. For "tradition," as such, meant nothing to them and they considered that the Universe was theirs to explore and to exploit as they saw fit and that it was their duty to submit all experience to the acid test of human intelligence.

Soon therefore they passed beyond those boundaries which the ancient world had accepted as impassable barriers—a sort of spiritual Mountains of the Moon. Then they turned against their former masters and within a short time a new and vigorous civilization replaced the out-worn structure of the ancient Asiatic world.

But of these Indo-Europeans and their adventures I give you a detailed account in "The Story of Mankind," which tells you about the Greeks and the Romans and all the other races in the world.

A FEW DATES CONNECTED WITH
THE PEOPLE OF THE ANCIENT WORLD

I can not give you any positive dates connected with Prehistoric Man. The early Europeans who appear in the first chapters of this book began their career about fifty thousand years ago.

THE EGYPTIANS

The earliest civilization in the Nile Valley developed forty centuries before the birth of Christ.
3400 B.C. The Old Egyptian Empire is founded. Memphis is the capital.

2800—2700 B.C. The Pyramids are built.

2000 B.C. The Old Empire is destroyed by the Arab shepherds, called the "Hyksos."

1800 B.C. Thebes delivers Egypt from the Hyksos and becomes the center of the New Egyptian Empire.

1350 B.C. King Rameses conquers Eastern Asia.

1300 B.C. The Jews leave Egypt.

1000 B.C. Egypt begins to decline.

700 B.C. Egypt becomes an Assyrian province.

650 B.C. Egypt regains her independence and a new State is founded with Sais in the Delta as

its capital. Foreigners, especially Greeks, begin to dominate the country.

525 B.C. Egypt becomes a Persian province.

300 B.C. Egypt becomes an independent Kingdom ruled by one of Alexander the Great's generals, called Ptolemy.

30 B.C. Cleopatra, the last princess of the Ptolemy dynasty, kills herself and Egypt becomes part of the Roman Empire.

THE JEWS

2000 B.C. Abraham moves away from the land of Ur in eastern Babylonia and looks for a new home in the western part of Asia.

1550 B.C. The Jews occupy the land of Goshen in Egypt.

1300 B.C. Moses leads the Jews out of Egypt and gives them the Law.

1250 B.C. The Jews have crossed the river Jordan and have occupied Palestine.

1055 B.C. Saul is King of the Jews.

1025 B.C. David is King of a powerful Jewish state.

1000 B.C. Solomon builds the Great Temple of Jerusalem.

950 B.C. The Jewish state divided into two Kingdoms, that of Judah and that of Israel.

900-600 B.C. The age of the great Prophets.

722 B.C. The Assyrians conquer Palestine.

586 B.C. Nebuchadnezzar conquers Palestine.
The Babylonian captivity.
537 B.C. Cyrus, King of the Persians, allows the
Jews to return to Palestine.

167-130 B.C. Last period of Jewish
independence under the Maccabees.

63 B.C. Pompeius makes Palestine part of the
Roman Empire.

40 B.C. Herod King of the Jews.

70 A.D. The Emperor Titus destroys Jerusalem.

MESOPOTAMIA

4000 B.C. The Sumerians take possession of the
land between the Tigris and the Euphrates.

2200 B.C. Hammurapi, King of Babylon, gives
his people a famous code of law.

1900 B.C. Beginning of the Assyrian State, with
Nineveh as its capital.

950-650 B.C. Assyria becomes the master of
western Asia.

700 B.C. Sargon, the ruler of the Assyrians,
conquers Palestine, Egypt and Arabia.

640 B.C. The Medes revolt against the Assyrian
rule.

530 B.C. The Scythians attack Assyria. There are revolutions all over the Kingdom.

608 B.C. Nineveh is destroyed. Assyria disappears from the map.

608-538 B.C. The Chaldeans reestablish the Babylonian Kingdom.

604-561 B.C. Nebuchadnezzar destroys Jerusalem, takes Phoenicia and makes Babylon the center of civilization.

538 B.C. Mesopotamia becomes a Persian province.

330 B.C. Alexander the Great conquers Mesopotamia.

THE PHOENICIANS

1500-1200 B.C. The city of Sklon is the chief Phoenician center of trade.

1100-950 B.C. Tyre becomes the commercial center of Phoenicia.

1000-600 B.C. Development of the Phoenician colonial Empire.

850 B.C. Carthage is founded.

586-573 B.C. Siege of Tyre by Nebuchadnezzar. The city is captured and destroyed.

538 B.C. Phoenicia becomes a Persian province.

60 B.C. Phoenicia becomes part of the Roman Empire.

A PERSIAN ALTAR.

THE PERSIANS

At an unknown date the Indo-European people began their march into Europe and into India.

The year 1000 B.C. is usually given for Zarathustra, the great teacher of the Persians, who gave an excellent moral law.
650-B.C. The Indo-European Medes found a state along the eastern boundaries of Babylonia.

550-330 B.C. The Kingdom of the Persians. Beginning of the struggle between Indo-Europeans and Semites.

525-8.C. Cambyses, King of the Persians, takes Egypt.

520-485 B.C. Rule of Darius, King of the Persians, who conquers Babylon and attacks Greece.

485-465 B.C. Rule of King Xerxes, who tries to establish himself in eastern Europe but fails.

330 B.C. The Greek, Alexander the Great, conquers all of western Asia and Egypt and Persia becomes a Greek Province.
The ancient world which was dominated by Semitic peoples lasted almost forty centuries. In the fourth century before the birth of Christ it died of old age.

Western Asia and Egypt had been the teachers of the Indo-Europeans who had occupied Europe at an unknown date.

In the fourth century before Christ, the Indo-European pupils had so far surpassed their teachers that they could begin their conquest of the world.

The famous expedition of Alexander the Great in 330 B.C. made an end to the civilizations of Egypt and Mesopotamia and established the supremacy of Greek (that is European) culture.

www.ingramcontent.com/pod-product-compliance
Lightning Source LLC
Chambersburg PA
CBHW020023030726
47499CB00007B/2245

* 9 7 8 3 7 3 2 6 2 3 1 9 8 *